I0544389

As
Fairydust Settles

by
Jansina

Cover Model: Joanna

Editor: Emilie of Rivershore Books

Medical Consultant: Ellen

Pea Little Ducky and *Pea Cari* fonts used with
permission from www.kevinandamanda.com/fonts

Handwritten note backgrounds used with
permission from Marisa Lerin of
www.pixelscrapper.com

Thank you!

As Fairydust Settles

Rivershore Books

ISBN: 0615933017
ISBN-13: 978-0615933016

Acknowledgments

To the long list of kindred spirits who listened, read various drafts, asked "When will your next book be finished?", and gave input: Thank you.

Your continued enthusiasm keeps my pen moving.

Simon Benson

Seven, five, and barely two. Those were the ages of my children when I became their only parent.

There had been so many words meant to encourage; trying to show sympathy. I can't remember even one. There were so many apologies—but no one was at fault.

No one but God.

Mical Blake

Fairytales never tell you what happens after "happily ever after." It's implied, of course.

It's a lie, of course.

Those stories had one thing in common with ours: The princes hardly knew who their princesses really were.

Chapter 1

Perhaps happily ever after was never meant to happen for me. Davey was surprised by the thought, yet it made sense. He tried to focus on the dry sandwich he was preparing for his lunch, but it was difficult with Mical's question still hanging in the air.

He watched his wife as she sat, studying, on the bed. Her back was hunched and she cradled her textbook in her lap, her legs resting over the edge. Mical's dark hair stubbornly fell forward, refusing to stay in place behind her ears. She turned another page, but her eyes drifted to him.

She was waiting for a response. *Would you have married me if you had known?*

Davey put the half-prepared sandwich in a bag and grabbed an apple, placed them both in his briefcase, and moved to the door. He rubbed one of his eyes, but not from lack of sleep. "What do you expect me to say?"

Her eyes narrowed and she shifted position, laying with her back to him and her eyes on the book. "Nothing, David. Just go. You're good at that."

"That's not fair, Mical." Davey set his briefcase down and leaned one arm against the doorframe.

Mical didn't move, and as she spoke he could hear her voice starting to shake. "You leave, every day, to be with *that man*."

Davey shook his head, trying to keep the frustration out of his own voice. "That man is your father, Mical."

She snorted. "He's my father in name only. You of all people should understand that."

He did understand, but he wasn't willing to give up the possibility of reconciliation. Sometimes her father seemed apologetic—loving, even. He couldn't let her throw that away. Not even if it hurt her, hurt him, and hurt their marriage to get to it. "My father didn't raise me, Mical. Yours did."

Mical turned her head to glare at him. "Do you really not hear the idiocy in that statement? So because he stuck around when I was little, that makes everything he's done since okay? Our situations aren't that different, only *I* didn't run. You're the one who always said that what he did was wrong." She lowered her head to her textbook once more, but she continued: "I suppose I should be grateful that he didn't send me to the streets. That's what you're saying, isn't it?"

Davey's voice was quiet as he shifted his weight to his other leg. "You know I don't believe that."

"Then why, Davey?" Mical turned completely around, drawing her legs up onto the bed and hugging her knees. Her textbook slipped, unwanted, to the floor. "Why do you feel so indebted to him?"

Davey frowned at her back. "He paid for our wedding..." It was a weak excuse. He didn't have a real answer for her—at least, not one she was open to hearing.

She snorted loudly. "He knew you would see it as a debt you owed! Don't you see how conniving he is?"

Davey didn't respond.

"Oh, that's right." The words started harshly, but Mical's tone softened into almost an apology as she continued. "I'm worse."

"I didn't say that." Davey shook his head.

"You didn't really have to, though, did you?" Mical turned and watched him, waiting for his response. She was waiting, really, for him to tell her everything was okay; for him to say that he forgave her, and they could go back to the way things had first been.

Davey picked up his briefcase. "I'm going to be late."

Mical was silent, resting her chin on her knees and staring at nothing in particular.

He watched her for a moment, then shook his head as if to remove the image and walked out.

The ride to Mr. Benson's was purposefully quiet. The peppy song on the radio annoyed him after only a few seconds, so he shut it off and stewed.

Not even a month into their marriage, Davey learned the truth. Although Mical had put on a believable show, she had never loved God as she had claimed to. When pressed, Mical mocked Davey's Papa as a heavenly being that was only real in the imaginations of the weak. She restrained herself for his sake, keeping her opinions to herself unless questioned, but that didn't change the facts. Mical had lied.

Worse, Davey had believed her.

Did I want it to be true so badly that I let myself be blind? Would You have stopped me if I had been listening, Papa? Davey had tried to live with no regret. He had made mistakes in the past, and he had overcome them. This was different. He had to live with the effects of his choices every day.

He pulled into Mr. Benson's driveway. The familiar, yet always foreboding, mansion was almost a comforting sight. He knew what to expect from this place.

Jonathan came to the door at Davey's knock. "I don't think you should be here," he said, glancing uneasily behind as he stepped outside and closed the door.

"What are you talking about, Jonathan?"

Jonathan looked up toward his father's office before responding to Davey's question. "Dad is in a mood today."

Davey rolled his eyes. "He's always in a mood." He smiled slightly, but the crease of concern didn't leave Jonathan's forehead.

"This is...different," he hesitated. "I overheard him. He's—he's planning something."

"I don't think it's good for you to read quite so many novels, little bro," Davey said, still unconcerned. Mr. Benson was also always planning something. "It probably isn't good for you to eavesdrop, either, if it ignites your imagination like this." The corners of Davey's mouth moved upward.

Jonathan's eyes narrowed. "This is serious, Davey!"

He shook his head, pushing past Jonathan to get to the door. "Your father hired me to update the security system, and I won't be leaving until that's finished."

Jonathan reached for the handle and held the door closed. "I don't want to see you hurt."

Davey's smile left his eyes. "There is nothing more he could do to me."

"Things can always be worse, Davey."

4

The corners of Davey's mouth fought to stay down. "I liked you better when you were unstoppably optimistic."

Still, Jonathan was unaffected. "Sometimes it's more important to face reality."

Davey crossed his arms and his words came quickly. "Okay—here's reality: Your father has already tried to dig up dirt on me and came up empty. He's messed with my personal life and failed, and he's too smart to make it a physical battle. There is nothing he can do that he hasn't already tried."

Jonathan's gaze was unfaltering. "Do you really know my father that little?"

Davey frowned, and his voice softened in concern. "You are always welcome to stay with Mical and me, or with my parents. I'm sure Mira and Aiden would welcome you. You don't have to stay here."

Jonathan spoke through his teeth: "I'm fine."

His concern evaporated. "Well, so am I." Davey stepped around Jonathan again, placing a hand on the door handle.

Jonathan hesitantly stepped aside and closed the door after Davey. "Please be careful."

"I don't need your conspiracy theories for that."

Jonathan followed him to the vault. "I'm not the type to offer conspiracy theories, and you know it."

Davey glared at Jonathan as he started to unlock the second door. The first, which required Mr. Benson's fingerprint and eye scan, had been propped open already.

"What is your problem today?"

Davey pressed the code, hit a wrong number and refreshed, then put it in again. "I don't have a problem."

"Right." Jonathan crossed his arms. "That's why you're treating the number pad like it's your personal punching bag."

Davey slammed the cover over the number pad and turned to Jonathan. "Did you know?"

He stepped back slightly. "What?"

Davey's eyes caught Jonathan's. "Did you know Mical was faking—all of it?"

Jonathan shook his head. "Not before you did."

"She's your *sister*. Didn't you have suspicions?" Davey scowled. "You knew her stubbornness. You had to know her transformation was unrealistic."

"As if you didn't. I wanted to believe as much as you did, so I didn't question." Jonathan pushed the vault door open. "It's done, Davey. I thought you were letting it pass."

"Maybe I can't." He walked to the next door in the vault, and reached for the electronic key. "This isn't something minor, Jonathan. My faith is the most important thing to me. She knew that."

"Yes," Jonathan continued cautiously, "but don't you understand why she did it?"

Davey scowled at the door, which was choosing not to recognize the key. "So it was okay to lie."

"No." Jonathan's tone was firm. "Mical was wrong." He stepped in and took the key from Davey, patiently placing it over the correct spot. "Try to see it from her perspective, though. The only way you would accept her was if she claimed to be a Christian...so she did."

Davey said nothing, so Jonathan continued. "It wasn't right, but it was understandable, in a way."

"Is that what you're doing with Chrissy?" Davey snapped as he tried pushing the third door open.

"Keep Chrissy out of this," Jonathan said, narrowing his eyes.

"Answer the question." The third door groaned but refused to open. Davey pulled a flashlight from his tool belt and started examining it.

"This isn't about me. It's about you. It's about my sister, and how she deserves to be treated. It was *you* who helped me see how wonderful God was. If you had acted the way you are now, I doubt that would have happened."

Davey turned, accidentally shining the light in Jonathan's eyes. "What are you talking about?"

Jonathan held up a hand to block the glare.

"Sorry," Davey mumbled and turned his attention back to the malfunctioning door.

"I always admired you, you know."

"Well, this just got awkward."

Jonathan playfully shoved Davey in the shoulder. "I mean, I couldn't understand how you could see the way Dad treated you, know it was wrong, and still show him nothing but kindness and respect."

Davey said nothing.

"Why can't you treat my sister the same?"

"I do." Davey took out a screwdriver and started adjusting the door. "What do you know about it, anyway?"

"Not much," Jonathan admitted. "Mical doesn't open up with anyone—especially not her little brother."

"Nor should she. Stay out of it."

"I can't, Davey. Not when I see her like this. She's not happy."

"You're so keen on reality—welcome to it. Most people aren't happy." When his attempts to fix the door did nothing, Davey threw the screwdriver at the wall.

"Most *newlyweds* are."

Davey rolled his eyes, retrieving the tool from where it had landed. "I hardly think we qualify for that title, considering." He turned to the door again.

Jonathan shook his head. "You're making a mistake."

"No. I *made* a mistake. Now I'm dealing with it."

"You are not 'dealing with it'. You're making it worse!"

Davey cursed as the screwdriver slipped from his hand.

Jonathan crossed his arms.

Davey picked it up and continued his work. "How could I possibly be making it worse?"

"If you don't already know, no explanation from me is going to change things."

"Perhaps not, but you wouldn't have mentioned it if you didn't want to chew me out. This is your chance to do that."

Jonathan turned away.

Davey worked in silence.

"I know your word is important to you," Jonathan finally said. "I know that's the only thing keeping you with Mical. She knows it, too."

"What's your point, Jonathan?"

"Marrying my sister was not a mistake. Don't you see how much she's changed? At least Mical is trying."

"She lied. Repeatedly. She manipulated me, you—all of us. Because she wanted her happily ever after. Is it my fault I'm not what she thought? I can't forgive her for this. Not yet."

Jonathan's lips drew together in frustration. "You believe marriage is for life, right?"

"That *is* what I signed up for when I said 'I do.'"

"You also believe that doesn't change, even when one or both people make a mistake."

"Of course it doesn't."

"So now you feel you're stuck with Mical, because you can't in good faith divorce her."

Davey shrugged. "Sure, if you want to put it that way."

"I'm putting it that way because that's how Mical feels. That's how you're *making* her feel."

"You think she deserves better?"

"It doesn't really matter what she deserves. You are called to love her in spite of *anything*. Because she's your wife; because she's a child of God; and

8

because she's been hurt enough without you adding to it."

Davey said nothing.

"You taught me that, Davey. At one point you
believed it—and lived it. Don't let the mistakes of
others change who you are." Jonathan watched
him for a moment, frowning at what he saw. "Or is
it too late for that already?" He shook his head and
walked out of the room.

Chapter 2

In sickness and in health, for richer or for poorer, for better or for worse, Mical let the words replay in her mind. In honesty and in deception weren't part of their promise.

Davey had no idea what he was agreeing to when he said 'I do.' Even without hearing his answer, Mical knew; Davey wouldn't have married her if he'd known.

She longed for the warmth she had when he was earning her love and trust. She wanted their love to be the only thing that mattered again.

It's too late.

Mical picked up her backpack and let it fall over one shoulder. Class wouldn't start for another two hours, but there was no reason to stay in the cottage. Every picture, every decoration, and even the house itself reminded her of everything Davey had given to be with her. It all reminded her of just how little she deserved it.

School was her own. She had it before Davey, and she would have it after, if it came to that.

Will it come to that?

She closed and locked the door. Her hand shook as she removed the key.

The walk to the bus stop was short, but cold. A Minnesotan winter had claimed the streets and sidewalks, making even a trip to the mailbox a risky venture. It was early November, but Mical had already lost count of the times she had slipped on the ice.

The driver, not the friendly one from her old route, gave an abrupt nod at her pass and shut the doors before she was up the stairs. Familiar faces greeted her with quiet indifference, and she walked past with the same.

In spite of her occasional frustrations with him, she missed having Peyton to sit beside. At least he initiated conversation. She would accept anything if it would help her avoid the thoughts her mind insisted on dredging up.

She sat in an empty area and pulled a textbook out of her bag. Her eyes scanned the words, but she let her mind wander to the conversations happening around her.

"Only two months now," a middle-aged woman commented.

Mical looked up in curiosity.

The woman's friend nodded with a smile, and placed a loving hand on her round belly.

Her eyes flicked to the book in her lap.

Another passenger made a half-hearted comment about the no good weather, to no one in particular. He received a small murmur of agreement in return.

A man three seats ahead spoke loudly into his cell: "What do you mean the email didn't send? I need this done *today*, Walters!"

The bus came to a stop, and a mother stepped on, her little girl holding tightly to her hand and sucking her spare thumb. Mical watched as they found an open seat and the girl climbed onto her mother's lap.

She turned to the window. The passing houses, trees, and buildings were less painful.

Why, when the hope of it has faded, should I want a child? Stupid, stupid heart.

"Are you all right?"

No, she wanted to say. *I am not all right, I am all wrong.*

Instead, she nodded slightly at the stranger across the aisle and turned to the front of the bus.

The next stop was hers, so she shoved her unread book into her bag, crossed her arms, and waited.

When the bus stopped moving, she hurried out into the cold once again. She quickly headed inside, and found her favorite study area. Tucked behind a back staircase were a comfy chair and a table, with a small lamp that almost gave enough light.

Since most students sought socialization, they headed to the main areas in the school to get it. Those had plenty of seating and ample lighting— unlike this this lone chair. It was seldom occupied.

Mical sat down, dropping her bag beside the chair, and turned on the light. She took a moment to just breathe.

I love this place. The building was warm compared to the outdoors, but still cool enough for a sweater. Nearby, students walked the halls in varying speeds. Some sat at a pair of benches, waiting for classes to start or friends to arrive while they pretended to study. Occasionally they talked

13

amongst themselves, usually in failed attempts at hushed tones—quieter than normal, but loud enough that an eavesdropper wouldn't have to strain.

It was busier and noisier than a library, but especially in Mical's area it sometimes reminded her of one. People were respectful there. Obnoxious cell phone conversations never occurred, and the conversations that did take place were seldom louder than necessary.

Sufficiently relaxed, she took her textbook and a highlighter out of the bag and began to truly focus on the words.

"I knew I'd find you here."

Mical looked up and smiled.

Anna sat on the ground, facing Mical. She crossed her legs and propped her elbows on her knees as she leaned forward. "How's it going?"

Mical glanced up at the clock on the far wall. When she squinted slightly, she could see that she still had almost half an hour before class. "Okay."

"What's wrong?"

She bit her lip. Somehow, Anna always knew.

Anna mistook her silence for reluctance. "I'm sorry...I know you come to this spot for the quiet."

Mical shook her head. "It's not that. I'm just not sure how to put it into words right now."

She nodded understandingly. "Do you want to go for coffee?"

"No," Mical said slowly. "I mean, I do, but I have class..."

"When are you done today?" Anna pulled out her phone and her eyes studied the screen.

"Two forty," Mical said, glancing again at the clock, though only a few minutes had passed.

"Great. I'm done at two. I'll meet you then." Anna typed something into her phone and leaned to the left as she put it back in her pocket. "You'll be in Business Economics, right?"

She nodded.

"What do you think of that class?"

Mical considered. "It's not the most exciting material...but I can see how it will apply later on."

Anna smiled. "I really don't know how you do it, Mically."

She closed her textbook, using the highlighter as a bookmark, and focused her attention on Anna. "Do what?"

"You treat everything so positively. It's inspiring."

Mical almost laughed. Clearly, Anna had a lot to learn about her.

Anna bounced to her feet. "I promised Peyton I'd give him my notes before class starts today." She shook her head a little, placing her right leg behind her left in a dance-like pose. "That boy really needs to start showing up more."

Mical watched her, curious. "He hasn't been coming?"

"He does sometimes. Sometimes he doesn't. Peyton's always been unpredictable about that kind of thing. I never can tell how serious he is about school."

Mical nodded. She'd noticed the same from him: a sometimes flippant attitude toward the classes, which could just as quickly change into a strong desire to do well. Neither truly fit what she knew of his personality.

"I'll see you outside your classroom at 2:40, Mically. Have a great day!" Anna twirled on her left foot and walked to the student center.

Mical's classes passed slowly, with her professors spending the majority of the time lecturing. Economics and business in general didn't lend itself to much discussion, and that was exactly what Mical preferred. Being presented with hard facts was a welcome change from the gray area the rest of her life had become.

As promised, Anna stood outside the classroom and grabbed Mical's arm as she exited. "Are you ready for some liquid warmth?"

She smiled and followed her to a nearby coffee shop.

Anna paused a moment before heading inside. Her eyes wandered around the street, and a smile reached them. "I just love this time of year." She held the door for Mical, grinning at her as she passed through.

Mical walked inside, rubbing her hands together for warmth. There was a line in the shop three or four people long. "Really?"

"Oh, yes. Christmas is coming!"

She shrugged, not nearly as excited by the holiday that was still more than a month away. Christmas had only been special for Mical when she was a child—when her mom was around. The first year without her mom, she had expected something from her dad. She was almost six, and not old enough to understand why there was no tree, no presents, and no joy.

Mira tried after that, but as an eight year old, she wasn't good at picking out gifts—and had no opportunities to buy them. Mical had been given Jonathan's socks, fruit she'd seen her father put in the fridge hours before, and several of her sister's dolls, which she promptly returned to their places in Mira's room.

Anna laughed lightly, still enraptured by her surroundings. "The world seems so much more kind during Christmas."

"If you say so," Mical mumbled in response. She turned her attention to the menu, though she already knew what her order would be. Her phone buzzed once in her pocket, but she ignored it.

Anna's gaze followed her own, and she smiled. "They have the ho ho mint mocha again. That's my favorite."

Mical nodded a little.

"What are you getting—do you know?"

"The campfire mocha," she responded.

"Mm...that's the one with the marshmallows, right?" Anna took a deep, appreciative breath. "That might be my second favorite."

Mical laughed.

Anna motioned her forward in the line, let her order, then told the clerk she was buying.

Mical opened her mouth to object, but Anna's grin stopped her. *Be gracious*, she reminded herself. It was something she was working on; one of many, in her attempt to be worthy of Davey—and of her friends. "Thank you, Anna."

"My pleasure," she said, leading Mical to the smaller counter where the drinks would be when they were ready. "Where shall we sit?"

She followed Anna's gaze around the small shop. The majority of the chairs were filled, including the coveted spot in front of the fireplace, but that was expected on cold afternoons like this one. She pointed to a small table on the side. The stools were taller there, and more difficult for someone Mical's height to be comfortable in, but she didn't see a better option.

"Perfect."

Yes, because it's one of the few that's unoccupied. Mical offered to collect the drinks if Anna wanted to claim it for them.

She glided to the table and placed her jacket on the back of her chair.

Mical stood awkwardly by the drink counter, waiting as those who had ordered before her were given their 'liquid warmth.' Finally, hers arrived.

Anna was on her phone again when Mical sat down. She slipped it into her pocket after a moment, and wrapped her hands around the cup. "Isn't this just the most delicious sensation?"

She fought to keep her eyebrow down, and smiled instead. The cup did feel wonderful on her cold hands.

"What's your favorite season, Mically?"

She considered. "Late spring. When all the flowers are out, and the weather is still cool."

Anna nodded slowly. "That's a beautiful time."

Mical could feel another text come through. *Who would be texting me?* She took a mental note of everyone who had her number. It was a short list: Anna, Chrissy, Davey, Peyton, and her family. No one in her family texted her, and Davey was hardly even on speaking terms. *It must be Chrissy or Peyton.*

Anna noticed her distraction, but didn't try to guess at the cause. "Do you have a favorite class this semester?"

Mical nodded, and began speaking animatedly about her Intro to Business Management course.

The afternoon passed much too quickly, as much-needed, though not incredibly deep, conversation filled the hours. When Mical finally glanced at her phone, it was past five.

The bus ride was quiet, until Mical's phone started to ring. *Jonathan?*

He didn't wait for her greeting. "Did you get my texts?"

"What? No. I mean, I guess. I didn't read them yet."

Jonathan let out a groan of frustration.

"Can't you just tell me what they said?"

"Not here. Just read them." He hung up.

Mical stared at her phone in confusion for a moment. The bus stopped and she had to quickly gather her things and head back to her house.

She gave herself a moment to let her hands warm up before starting supper. Davey would be home in just a few moments, and she liked having food for him when he came. It let him relax when he came back, instead of having to worry about cooking.

Still, she missed spending time with him in the kitchen.

He wouldn't want that, now.

As the bacon was beginning to heat up on the stove and the bread was browning in the toaster, she remembered Jonathan's call. She pulled up her texts:

Dad's planning something...not good.

Don't let Davey near Dad.

Mical shook her head. *What is that supposed to mean?* She replied:

Explain yourself.

Chapter 3

Mical was on her phone when Davey came inside. She slammed the phone down in frustration. She let a few curse words permeate the air before seeing him and realizing she wasn't alone in the house.

Even as angry as he was, Davey's expression softened when her eyes, filled with an emotion he had only seen once before, met his. "Mical?"

She lowered her gaze, guilty.

Davey stepped closer. *You have to love her in spite of everything. In spite of anything.* If he was honest, his love had never stopped. It had only ceased to be the most important thing about their relationship.

He wrapped his arms around her, frowning as he felt her shiver against him. "Was someone here?"

She shook her head, but gave no attempt to clarify the cause of her fear.

Davey turned the stove off and moved the slightly too brown bacon off the burner, then led her to the table and sat beside her. His arms slipped away from her, but he took her hands in his. "Please talk to me, Mically."

Her eyes found his, and pools of tears appeared, threatening to release at the slightest movement.

He forced his voice to be as gentle as he could make it. "What happened?"

With a shaky hand, she lifted her phone to him. It was opened to a short text conversation with Jonathan.

> **Jonathan:** Don't let Davey near Dad.
> **Mical:** Explain yourself.
> **Jonathan:** wants 2 blame him 4 crime. Needs fingerprints.
> **Mical:** I don't understand.
> **Jonathan:** jail or worse. Sent some guys.
> **Mical:** Go where I can call you.

That told him next to nothing. Jonathan was still playing into his wild imaginings—and apparently he was trying to pull Mical in with him.

More than trying; he had succeeded.

Davey looked at Mical once more. "Okay..." He tried to keep the skepticism out of his voice, but it was difficult. "Did he say anything else?"

She stood up, heading to the bedroom.

He watched without comprehension as she arranged some pillows underneath the sheets. "What are you doing?"

"They're coming for you."

Just play along. She needs this, I guess. "Who is?"

She frowned, sensing the amusement in his voice. "This is serious, David!"

His tone became gentle again as he saw the real fear Mical was once again struggling to hide. "I'm okay, Mical. I was just with your father. Look at me. I'm not hurt, I'm not in prison. That isn't going to change."

Mical moved more pillows around.

He stepped closer to her and took one of her hands in his, stopping the motion. "Your father has been making empty threats for months. He never truly means it. We're going to be okay."

She pulled her hand free and shook her head. "There is more to this than you think. Jonathan wouldn't have warned me if he didn't have a good reason. He doesn't do that."

Until today, I would have agreed with you.

"You need to do something to protect yourself."

"Do what, Mical?"

"Leave!"

Davey frowned. After a moment of silence, he asked softly, "Is that really what you would like?"

She nodded, but quickly shook her head seconds later. "Just for now—for this. Just so you are safe. I... I..." Her mouth closed, stopping the thought.

"What is it, Mical?"

"I don't want you hurt," she said.

Too late.

Still, her concern made him smile. He wrapped her in his arms once more, and kissed her forehead.

She let herself relax against him, but he could feel her heartbeat quicken when a pounding on the door interrupted them a moment later. "Go, Davey. Please," she said; her voice was no louder than a whisper.

Davey realized this would be the only way to calm her irrational fears. He nodded. "Okay, Mical. For you, I will do it." He tilted her chin up and kissed her softly.

She winced at first, but immediately tried to cover the expression with a nervous smile. "Davey, don't tell me where you're going, okay? When Father asks, I want to be able to answer truthfully."

He nodded slightly. He wouldn't go far, not even away from the house, but if it soothed her he'd keep quiet. He headed to the door.

"No!" Mical whispered it as loudly as she dared.

Davey paused, his hand still on the doorknob.

"The back," she said, speaking quietly but urgently. "Go out the back."

Davey nodded. Seeing how terrified she was, and knowing that she thought she was doing all this to protect him, he couldn't help but pause to give her a kiss before heading to the backyard. He held her gently in his arms for a moment, trying to calm her shaking body.

She pushed him toward the back door. "Please, Davey," she whispered, handing him a coat and boots.

He slipped outside, noting with slight interest that the pounding had gotten louder. *Whoever it is, they're sure in a hurry.* He shivered against the cold wind that blew snow on his uncovered arms, and quickly pulled on his coat. *But no wonder.*

She had closed and locked the door behind him, and he sat with his back against it. His coat was warm, for the moment, but he hoped whatever was going on inside wouldn't take long.

What was she hoping to accomplish with those pillows? He strained to listen, and for the first time was glad that the walls of the house were thin.

Mical had let the stranger inside, and Davey made out the low rumble of a man's voice. He concentrated on deciphering the words, and noted multiple sets of loud footfalls.

"We need to speak to David."

The floor boards creaked. Mical was pacing, or the men had begun to search the house.

"Davey's sick," Mical said.

At least I'm not the only one she finds it easy to lie to.

"That doesn't change the fact that we need to see him."

"He's asleep," she lied again, "and probably contagious."

Davey smirked. *Yes, scare them away with the possibility of germs.* He recognized one of the voices as belonging to Doug, one of the security guards at Mr. Benson's business.

The men were unabated. "Let us in, or we will force our way past you."

Davey blinked at the harsh words. *I just saw Doug today. What happened since I came home that caused such an emergency?*

There was silence, and he knew her well enough to guess that Mical was hesitating.

What is her plan now?

"I really wish you would let him be. He needs his rest."

"We will only be a moment, Miss Benson."

"I am *not* Miss Benson anymore, Ron," she said stiffly, automatically. Her tone softened. "Just call me Mical."

"If he is as sick as you say, Mical," Doug said, his tone reasonable, "we will leave him be and either come back later or wait for him to return to work."

He wondered what she was doing. Nodding silently, relenting and hoping for the best; standing her ground, refusing to let them in; or biting her lip, in that cute way she always did, and staying on the verge of a decision, biding her time in case it helped?

Helped what? There's nothing going on here. It's just a routine house call from work.

Davey blinked at the thought. *I've never had a 'routine house call' before.*

For a moment, he questioned if he was right to dismiss Mical's worry. Perhaps he should have listened to her and Jonathan. They had always been level-headed before, and were used to their father's antics even more than Davey was. Why had he doubted them?

Perhaps he should have gone farther than just the backyard.

No. Even if they were right, that would be a cowardly move. He should face the enemy, if it existed, head on, as he always had. He should be there for Mical. He should be there for his wife.

The floor boards creaked again, louder now. She had been nodding, then. The noises quieted in the area of the bedroom. *The pillows—she was using them...to look like me.* But they looked nothing like him; nothing at all like a person. They resembled only what they were: a pile of pillows.

Her lie would be found out...and her father would be angry. She knew that would happen, but she did it anyway. *She was protecting me.*

"You see?" She was forcing her voice to remain steady, but Davey knew her well enough to hear the tremors. "He is sleeping. I would like it to stay that way."

There was a momentary silence. Davey nearly charged inside, as his imagination created terrible scenarios of what the silence could mean.

"All right. Let's let him sleep," Ron said.

"We'll tell Mr. Benson," Doug's tone was apologetic. "We should have known not to doubt you."

...Are they blind?

He heard them leave, offering well wishes as they did so. His confusion grew. *Did she do something more to the pillows?* Doug and Ron weren't stupid. They would have seen right through that lumpy pile.

When the silence in the house assured him they had left, Davey walked to the unlocked front door and entered. He slipped off his boots, walked to the stove, and let his hands hover over the still-warm burner.

Mical, who had been looking blankly into a mug of coffee before he entered, stared at him, her face pale. "I-I thought you left. Why are you still here?"

Davey chuckled a little. "If I didn't know any better, I would think you didn't want me here."

"I told you to leave," she stood, starting to pace.

"Okay...so maybe you don't. I was in the backyard, and I heard everything. Now do you see there's nothing to be worried about?"

Mical frowned. "Momentarily, there isn't. That won't last."

"How did you convince them those pillows were me?" he asked as he walked to the bedroom.

The bed was still lumpy, but it resembled a person more than he remembered. He picked up the edge of the cover to see what was underneath: an almost life-size statue of Michaelangelo's *David*.

Another like it had a place in a corner of Mr. Benson's office. *Is this the same statue?* He knew Mr. Benson wouldn't have given it to Mical. *How did I never see it before? Am I that unobservant?*

"Mical...?" his voice was quiet as he tried to keep judgment out.

She scowled, seeing through his gentle approach. "Yes, that was my father's. I stole it."

"If you wanted, um, *David*, I could have gotten you one. Well, not this big of one, probably, but..."

Mical shook her head. "I hate that statue. I mean, it's not the statue. It's the principle of the thing."

Davey wasn't following her thought process. "The principle?"

She shrugged. "It's just one of the many things Father bought for himself—when he should have been caring for us. I just wanted to do something to hurt him. Just once. I wanted to see how it felt...I wanted to know..."

"You wanted to know why he did it...still does it."

She nodded. "Is that so terrible?"

Davey knew stealing was wrong. His past made him feel it even more acutely. Still, he knew why she had done it. She had been hurt numerous times by the man who was supposed to love her most until her "prince" came. Instead, she had been forced to play mother to herself and her siblings since she was five years old and had never been taught not to repay pain with pain.

He wasn't convinced that he was the best teacher for her, either. He had retaliated from her deception to give her a new kind of abuse: neglect. He was hurting, and he took it out on her. What she had done to her father was no different than what he had done to her. Whether they were justified in it made no difference; it was still wrong.

Mical didn't need a lecture at that moment. She needed understanding and love: things he had been reticent to give her since he learned the truth.

She looked up at him. Her voice was soft and shook with emotion. "I can return it to him...if you want. I don't want it here anyway."

He matched her tone. "It's okay, Mical. He doesn't seem to miss it right now." Davey tucked a stray hair behind her ear and kissed her forehead. "What's scaring you?" He sat down and patted the bed for her to join him.

She did, hesitantly. "They might return..."

"I know those men. I work with them every day, or at least see them. They don't frighten me. Why do they frighten you?"

"Because they're here to do what my father wants them to," she said. "It's not Doug and Ron that scare me—it's what they could do to you. They're here to gather evidence to frame you for murder."

Davey's eyebrows went up. "How do they expect to do that?"

"They need your fingerprint. Jonathan said Father found or made something that transfers fingerprints, so they need you to touch it, and he can put it on whatever he wants." Mical rubbed her arm. "He's going to put it on a murder weapon."

Davey frowned. "I don't believe your father would murder someone just to mess with us, Mical. Surely you're mistaken."

"Jonathan isn't wrong often, Davey." She lowered her eyes and her voice quieted. "I don't think he's wrong this time. I trust him. You used to."

"I still do," Davey said, letting out a frustrated breath. "This just seems so...preposterous."

"It's no more preposterous than what he's already done to you."

"Mical, there is a big difference between trying to harm someone's reputation and trying to frame them for murder." He stood and paced in irritation. "Even if he wanted to and had a way to frame me, your father would *not* kill someone to do it."

"I guess you're right," Mical watched him for a moment. "He wouldn't go that far." She again lowered her eyes to her fidgety hands, but quickly looked up, a new fear on her face. "Maybe he wouldn't have to do the killing."

"What else, Mical?" Davey dropped his hands to his sides. "What else? Hire an actor to play dead? That wouldn't last long once cops showed up."

She shook her head. "Unsolved murders, Davey. They exist. I don't know how many, but he'd only need one... All my father would have to do is find a murder without a suspect, and then point in your direction. With your fingerprints on an identical weapon...you'd be arrested."

"That would work if the weapon was a knife...but I think most people are killed with guns—and those can be traced."

"Money can do a lot of things that shouldn't be possible, Davey."

That, at least, was true. *But Mr. Benson has no reason to do it.*

"It would only have to be for a little while, Davey."

He turned to her. "What would?"

She blinked, as if unsure how to explain what she meant. "I—I mean—I don't want you to be hurt, so..."

He understood. "You want me to leave. Really leave."

She nodded; her eyes examined the floor.

"For...how long?"

"I'll tell you when it's safe."

You mean you'll tell me when you've stopped being paranoid. How long will that take?

"Go, Davey. Please. Go to someone you trust."

Davey wrapped his arms around Mical and kissed her gently. *Okay; for you.* "I will, Mical."

She held him for a moment. "I love you, Davey."

He didn't return the words; he wasn't ready for that. He hoped she knew anyway.

She looked up at him and kissed him.

She knows.

Mical slipped something into his pocket, then ushered him outside.

He would go. To give her peace, he would go. But where?

Sammy. He needed the wisdom he knew Sammy would offer. Not for Mical and Jonathan's imaginings...but for his marriage.

Chapter 4

Mical looked critically at her makeshift replacement for Davey. The pillows made it lumpy, and the little you could see of the head was clearly too pale and stiff to belong to a living human being.

Are father's employees really that unobservant, or are they, somehow, on my side in this? Surely they would not have risked their jobs simply to protect Davey. *Would they?*

Mical began to relax at the realization that this was, perhaps, over. Her shoulders tensed a moment later. *This probably won't be over for quite some time. Davey...please be safe. Please.*

She set Davey's phone on the nightstand and tried to rearrange the blankets, pillows, and replica statue of Michaelangelo's *David* in a way that looked more like an actual person. She was grateful Doug and Ron had let her deception go so quickly, but she knew her father would not.

I deserve whatever my father has in mind for me. Not for this...but for everything else—for hurting Davey.

Even if she didn't, it would still be worth it. She would do anything to protect her husband.

Davey...do you know how much I love you?

She tried to think of a way to create the illusion of breathing, but it was clear her brain was not talented in that area. The lump in the bed would have to be enough. It would stall her father if only for a moment, and that would have to suffice. *Please, Davey, get away quickly.*

When pacing, studying, and cooking supper only served to make her more nervous, she moved instead to her computer.

Peyday: There you are. Thought you had died or something ;)
Mically: Cute
Peyday: Missed you after class
Mically: Yeah. I was busy
Peyday: Doing what?
Mically: Doesn't matter
Peyday: Okay... Don't forget that paper is due tomorrow, princess
Mically: ...What paper?
Peyday: Just making sure you're paying attention. There's no paper
Mically: You are a jerk
Peyday: I try ;)
Mically: Why does that not surprise me?
Peyday: *shrugs*

Mical glanced at the chat list, hoping to see Chrissy's name or Anna's. Peyton was the only one online.

Peyday: Hang out after class tomorrow?
Mically: Find someone else to stalk, Peyton
Peyday: It's not stalking if you know it's happening
Mically: … That's wrong.
Peyday: So, really, where were you today?
Mically: With Anna
Peyday: So descriptive. Doing what?
Mically: Minding my own business
Peyday: Subtle

She closed the chat window and looked at the buddy list again. *Thank goodness.*

Mically: You there?
AnnaBear: Hey Mical

Another window popped up.

Peyday: You're not usually quite so dodgy
Mically: I'm not dodging
Peyday: You're distracted
Mically: *shrugs*
Peyday: I'm not used to people not giving me their full attention

She rolled her eyes and closed his chatbox again. Anna had said nothing more.

Mically: You seem quiet today

Still nothing.
Mical frowned and glanced at her textbooks. *I really need to focus.*
A quiet bell told her Peyton's window had popped up again.
Seriously? Take a hint!

Peyday: Now you're just being rude

Mical scowled. She right clicked his name and let her curser hover over the "delete" option.

That'll make class awkward on Monday.

She groaned, but didn't click. *Some other time, perhaps.* The thought made her smile.

Mically: I don't feel like dealing with your crap today, Peyton
Peyday: You used to love my crap

...When?

Mically: I used to *tolerate* your crap
Peyday: :(You are a meaniepants
Mically: You are a two year old. Learn English
Peyday: Aww
Mically: Just leave me alone. I have no patience for you today

She closed it once more, pressing harder than necessary on the touchpad. She reached for her coffee as she brought Anna's chat window back to the front.

Mical typed with one hand as she sipped her cold drink.

Mically: Everthig okay?

Oops.

AnnaBear: Yah
Mically: Are you sure?
AnnaBear: Are you talking to Peyton?

Mical bit her lip, not sure how to respond—or why it mattered.

Mically: I was

Anna is typing...

After waiting at least a minute for Anna's message, the words disappeared; she had deleted it without sending. *What is she afraid to tell me?*

Mically: Why?
AnnaBear: Just asking
Mically: Because...?

Anna said nothing.

Mical frowned. She picked up her cell phone, hoping for a message of some sort: a reassurance that everything was okay. She had no new notifications.

Why didn't I let him take his phone? I knew where it was, and I purposely kept it here.

She knew why. Her father would track it if he'd had it. *At least he's safe...for now. Right?*

Mically: You can tell me
AnnaBear: Just be careful
Mically: What?
AnnaBear: Don't lead him on. He likes you

She shook her head. *He just pretends to—he's not serious.* Why couldn't Anna see that?

Mically: I think you're wrong
AnnaBear: Let's hope for that

Peyton's window popped up again.
Are you kidding me?

Peyday: Will you have patience to deal with me tomorrow?
Mically: Sure. Whatever.

Peyday: Don't tell me you forgot about our study session

Sorry. I've had more important things on my mind.

Mically: I'll be there
Peyday: :)

She closed the window again.

AnnaBear: Hey, I've got to go
Mically: Okay
AnnaBear has signed off

Mical jumped in surprise as the door slammed shut.

"Micaela Serie Benson!"

He's here. She'd known he would come, but she still wasn't ready. *I'll never be ready to deal with that man.*

She closed her laptop and let out a long breath before joining him at the front door.

"Hello, Father."

Mr. Benson walked past her, through the living room, and into the hall. "Where is he?" He walked into the bedroom and yanked the covers off the bed. A string of swear words escaped his mouth.

This is my home. He has no right. Mical watched him, leaning against the doorway for support. She could feel her throat tighten, but she forced the tears to stay down. *This was my safe place.*

He turned to her, and the cursing became directed.

She looked down as it continued.

Her father spat the words. "Where is he?"

"I don't know," she whispered, and motioned to his phone, sitting on the dresser. "He left in a hurry."

"Why would you do this?" Her father picked up the pillows and threw them across the room, as if he was hoping to find Davey hiding underneath. His voice grew louder as he saw the statue in Davey's place. "Why would you deceive your own father?"

"He told me to," she lied. She rubbed her arm to keep it from shaking visibly. "What is this about?"

He looked at her in disgust and turned away, muttering under his breath all the filth Mical had been trying to keep out of her house.

Mical took a deep breath. *Maybe if I'm quiet, he'll just leave.*

He didn't. Instead, he snatched Davey's phone, knocking down at least three knickknacks that had been beside it.

Her fists balled. "Don't *touch* that!" she screamed, her voice reaching a rare pitch as she lunged forward.

The surprise of her attack caused her father to drop the phone. The back separated and the battery popped out when it hit the ground.

"What the—"

"No!" she yelled, her eyes becoming slits as she collected the phone's pieces. When she lived with him, perhaps that was acceptable. Not in her home.

He crossed his arms and tapped his foot.

"You need to leave," she said, surprised at the strength in her own voice. "Right now."

He laughed. "And why would I do that?"

Mical's eyebrows drew together. *You couldn't make this easy, could you, Father?* "You're trespassing," she said.

"I'm family." His chin tilted upwards and he gave a smug, almost smile.

"Why don't we see how the cops interpret the situation?" She pulled out her own phone and started to dial seven random numbers. *Let this be enough.* She hit the "send" button and held the phone to her ear. It started to ring.

"We're not done here," her father said, but went to the door. "This isn't over."

She moved the phone away from her ear as someone on the other end picked up.

"Goodbye, Father."

She locked it behind him, her heart beating quickly.

"Hello?"

Mical held the phone up to her ear. "Wrong number—sorry. And...thank you." She sat on the kitchen tile, her back against the door. She let the phone drop into her lap and covered her face with her shaking hands.

After more than five minutes of uninterrupted tears, she returned to her computer.

She opened a blank Word document as she waited for chat to load. A window popped up as soon as she was logged on.

Peyday: Don't believe in goodbyes now?
Mically: I'm inviting Anna to join us tomorrow
Peyday: That's cool. I like Anna

Mical smiled. She tried to picture Anna and Peyton together, but quickly shook her head. Peyton didn't deserve Anna.

That wasn't it. It was more that no one deserved to be stuck with Peyton.

Peyday: So, meet right after class?
Mically: Yah
Peyday: See you then. Bye! (See? I use them)
Mically: Whatever
Peyday has signed off

Mical rolled her eyes. *This paper is not going to be written today,* she admitted to herself.

She picked up her plate. A pile of cold macaroni and cheese sat untouched in the center. She picked at it with her fork, with no real intention of eating it.

After playing with her food a few more minutes, she scraped it into a container and stored it in the fridge.

Davey's gone. He's safe. Father can't frame him now.

She went back to the bedroom and arranged the pillows on the bed, stuffing the extras into the closet. With some difficulty, she moved the statue of *David* into the spare room, wondering if her father had realized it was his. That had obviously not been his focus.

She grabbed her backpack and headed to the bedroom. A few moments later, she was huddled under the covers, trying to focus on Business Economics.

Hours later, her textbook doubled as a pillow.

After class the next day, Mical, Peyton, and Anna gathered in the student area to study.

Anna sat on the table, knees tucked under her chin, as Mical hunched over her notes and read out loud. Peyton was sprawled on the floor in front of them, doodling in the margins of his textbook as he held it above his head.

"What—that's not what the book says." Peyton rolled onto his stomach and flipped through to find the right section.

Mical let out a frustrated breath. "I *know*—but it's what Professor Jenson said, and since it's not the book that's grading my test, that's what I'm going with."

Anna glanced from Mical to Peyton.

"Would you rather get an A, or would you rather be right?"

"I'd rather have the A."

Peyton scowled.

"Okay, I declare a study break," Anna said. "Let's go to the cafeteria."

"I'm out," Peyton said.

Anna frowned. "Now you're just *trying* to be difficult."

"Doesn't take much," Mical muttered.

"Maybe I just don't care for nasty cafeteria food."

Anna hopped off the table, narrowly avoiding Peyton's legs. "Watch our stuff, Mr. Crabbypants," she ordered.

He shrugged in response.

"Like anyone is going to steal boring business books," Peyton muttered.

Anna laughed.

The girls picked out plates of salad, and Anna bought a piece of fried fish and a bag of chips for Peyton. "He might change his mind when he sees it," she answered Mical's questioning look. "Besides, he's only cranky because he's hungry."

"If you say so."

"Now don't *you* get cranky. I can only handle one of you at a time." She playfully elbowed Mical.

"I'm not cranky."

"Why'd you ask me to come today? I mean, we only share two classes—and neither are the one you have a major test in."

"Well...you said to be careful with Peyton, and I don't really know the others in that class yet." She watched Anna. "Do you mind terribly?"

Anna shook her head. "Not at all. If you have to study with him, I'm happy to balance things out for you. I wonder, though, if you might be better off studying on your own."

Mical shrugged. "You're probably right."

"Why did you agree to it?"

"Honestly? I'm not sure why I do a lot of things these days." Mical sighed.

Anna set her tray on a table. "Talk."

Mical wanted to. *I can't tell her. At least, not here.* She shrugged as she set her own tray next to Anna's. "I'm just stressed with school."

Her friend's pursed lips showed Mical had been unconvincing, but Anna said nothing.

Chapter 5

Davey felt in his pocket, searching again for his phone. *Guess I forgot it at home.* He turned down the road in the direction of Sammy's cabin.

The elderly man was sitting in his recliner, facing the window, and reading the newspaper. He folded the paper and laid it across his lap as Davey pulled into the driveway.

With some effort, Sammy stood and waited by the door for him. He greeted him with a hug. "Davey!" He glanced toward the truck. "No Mical?"

"Not this time, Sammy," Davey said, returning the firm hug.

Sammy released him, but kept his hands on Davey's shoulders and looked him in the eyes. "I would really like to get to know your darling wife one of these days." His eyes squinted slightly as he watched Davey. "You know that, right?"

"Yes, Sammy," Davey said, chuckling. "You only remind me of it every time we talk."

Sammy shook his head as he retrieved his cane from where it was leaning against the umbrella rack. "And yet you are here alone, again. Explain?"

"I will—but...later."

Sammy stood in one place for a moment, seeming to catch his breath. "Your parents are here. At least, they were last night."

Davey laughed, enjoying the reminder of the easygoing relationship Sammy shared with his family. "I'll be right in," he said as Sammy returned to his chair.

Davey retrieved his bag from the passenger seat in his truck. *At least I remembered to pack some things.*

The cabin was warmer than Davey would have chosen, but it wasn't uncomfortable. He dropped his bag in the entryway and untied his boots.

He could see the kitchen in front of him, and smiled at the years of memories around that worn, wooden table. He and Robbie had many arguments there, and his family had almost always shared a second Thanksgiving meal with Sammy. "City folk" were too fancy for him, so he refused their invitations to join theirs, but always returned them with a request to have it at his cabin.

Sammy's place was only an hour from the cities—no farther than some suburbs were from each other—so he wasn't as much of a country man as he liked to pretend.

The uncle-figure had returned to his newspaper, a mug of tea in one hand.

"Anything good happening in the news today?" Davey asked.

Sammy shrugged. "Not yet. There will be, though. They always stick a couple positive things in—you just have to dig for them."

Davey chuckled.

"I *knew* I heard my boy's voice!" Ella walked up from the hall around the corner. His dad's head peered around the kitchen wall, and the rest of his body followed.

Hugs were passed around as well as more inquiries about Mical. Davey deflected them as well as he could.

"She asked me to leave," he said simply.

His mom hugged him again. "I love you, Davey."

He swallowed, realizing with a tightening throat just how long it had been since he had heard those words from someone he trusted.

"If I'd known asking is all it took, we would have gotten you out of our house years earlier," Joe chuckled.

Ella elbowed Joe, but a smile threatened the corners of her mouth.

Davey laughed. *Oh Dad, I've missed you.*

Joe gave his half smile, but it didn't last. "Did she give a reason?"

He nodded slowly, deciding how much to share. "She thinks she's protecting from her father."

"Protecting you...?"

Sammy looked up from his newspaper. "Davey, doesn't she know it's the men who do the protecting?"

"Well, Mical's never been traditional." He shrugged.

Ella crossed her arms. "Explain, David. What's going on?"

Joe moved to the kitchen as they waited for Davey to form words, and the others followed.

With help from Sammy, Joe gathered the ingredients he needed and began to cook.

Davey picked up a knife and started slicing a tomato. "Mical and I... We've been having some problems lately."

"I thought so," Ella said gently. She led him to the table and away from the cutting board. "Let Joe do that," she said. "You, tell me what has been happening."

Davey stiffened, as he always did when people asked about something he wasn't ready to discuss.

"Davey, I am your mother." She pulled her chair close to his and put an arm around him. "Please don't block me out."

He tried to find words.

Joe and Sammy left their cooking for a moment and sat on the other side of him.

"Did your mother and I ever tell you about what happened just a few days after we were married?" Joe asked.

Davey shrugged, but appreciated the change in subject. "I don't know; maybe."

"I think you would remember if we had," he grinned at Ella.

She removed her arm from Davey's shoulders. "I don't want that story told, Joe. Don't you have food to cook?"

"Darling, I really don't understand why you dislike this story so much," Joe said with a smile.

"It makes me sound like a demanding wife." She tucked her hair behind her ear self-consciously.

"Nonsense," he said. "And even if it did, we all know you well enough not to believe it."

"At the time I'm fairly certain you *did* believe that!"

"At the time," his dad said, smiling at the memory, "I was half asleep and would have thought *anyone* was a demanding wife...or, person in general. I suppose even in that state I wouldn't have thought that just anyone was my wife."

Davey's mom giggled. "I suppose you're right."

"So Ella, would you like to start?"

"Fine," she said, realizing Joe's stubborn nature had set in. She moved to the kitchen with the excuse that a pot was boiling over.

Davey hadn't heard it.

Keeping her focus on the stove, his mom began. "A few days after we were married, I told Joe I would buy blueberries if he would bake them into a pie."

"And of course I agreed—though, to be honest, I had no intention of baking it without help."

"Is that relevant?" Ella asked, stirring the pasta.

Joe shrugged, and joined her at the stove, dropping spices and the chunks of tomato Davey had started to cut into the sauce.

"So I went to the store," Ella said.

"While I took Davey to the park—"

"—without telling me."

"You weren't around."

Davey stood and found an onion to add to the sauce. He started cutting, trying not to breathe in too many of the fumes.

Sammy chuckled. "I suppose I should be grateful I never married."

"Oh, no, marriage is wonderful," Joe said. As if to emphasize his point, he kissed Ella on the cheek.

She blushed and pushed him away, but her smile betrayed her.

Davey took a break from cutting the onion to snatch up the last chunk of tomato before Joe could mix it with the sauce. He smiled. "I remember that day, a little."

Joe's tone became serious. "Oh, no," he said. "We've traumatized the boy." He shook his head sadly.

Davey laughed. "Actually, that was the day I discovered spiders."

"That orphanage sure kept you sheltered if you didn't know about spiders until you were five," Sammy said.

Joe chuckled. "The spiders in the sink—yes. Interesting what pieces stick out."

Satisfied that the pasta was ready, Ella took the spoon from Joe while he dumped the water and let the noodles drain.

"So, what happened next?" Sammy asked.

"Yes, darling," Joe said in a quiet, syrupy tone, "what happened next?"

Ella faced the stove as she continued. "I came home to an empty house. No note; nothing. So I threw the blueberries into the sink—I mean, really threw them—and went for a walk."

"To the cemetery, right?"

"Right."

Joe continued the story: "Davey and I came home and figured she was still gone." He moved the pasta into a bowl and helped Ella pour the sauce over it. "We'd been playing in the dirt at the park, so I helped him wash his hands and washed my own, then sent Davey to play."

"And neither one of them noticed the blueberries in the sink. They just let the dirt and bugs fall all over them."

"We're guys, dear. What else did you expect?"

"Well, I expected you to do what you said you would. When I came home, the pie had *still* not been made—and the blueberries were covered with dirt and spiders."

"So she had to yell at me."

"I had to."

Davey and Sammy set plates and glasses on the table as they listened. Joe brought the spaghetti as Ella filled a pitcher with water.

"Well, he wasn't thrilled about that."

Joe chuckled. "You put it so mildly, darling."

Ella smiled.

"I was mad," Joe admitted, "and took it out on my poor wife."

"Hardly. Well, okay...a little."

Joe chuckled. "And because she's so wonderfully sweet, she said she would make the pie instead."

Ella blushed. Unlike Joe, who did so at every possible moment—mainly because it bothered Ella and he loved to frustrate her—she never fished for compliments. Although Joe gave them often and freely, she was always caught off guard when they came.

She rarely gave them to him in return, and never without prompting—words of affirmation were not her strong point. The beauty in their situation was that Joe never needed to hear them.

Ella cleared her throat. "That isn't exactly how it went." She tucked an invisible strand of hair behind her ear. "I used those words...but not in a pleasant tone."

Joe smiled. "And I decided, since I didn't have to bake after all, I would take a nap."

"Oh dear," Sammy said.

"Now where were you when this was going on, Sammy? I sure could have used your guidance." He chuckled.

Ella nodded, remembering. "By the time the pie was ready, I had calmed down a bit, but when I found him sleeping I was upset again. I mean, you know I don't like cooking, especially not alone. So I woke him up. Like this." She tilted the pitcher of water above Joe's head.

"Hey!" He quickly dodged it. "They don't need a demonstration!"

"I bet he wasn't happy," Davey said between laughter.

"No, he wasn't. He rolled over, pulled the covers up over his head, and told me to go away...in not so nice terms."

"What? All I said was 'go away'!"

Ella shook her head. "I seem to remember it differently."

"Well in that case, you seem to remember it wrong."

Ella rolled her eyes with a smile.

"Either way, I was cranky. I hadn't slept well the night before, and had finally gotten past the 'I'm tired but can't stop thinking' stage." He turned to Davey with a slightly accusatory tone. "Your mother bursts in, not only disturbing my rest, but with an impatient air about her."

Ella frowned and crossed her arms. "And *this* is why I don't like this story being told—at least, not the way you tell it."

"I know you don't like the way I tell it, dear. That's why I let you be the storyteller this time."

"You did?"

"Yes, darling."

"Right now?"

Joe smiled innocently. "Yes, dear."

"It seems to me, sweetie, you are trying to take over."

"Nonsense! Davey, do you hear the nonsense coming out of this lovely lady's mouth?"

"Oh no," Davey held up his hands in defense. "You keep me out of this. I've seen what happens to people who find themselves in the middle of your squabbles. Poor souls never know what they are in for until it's too late."

Joe chuckled. "Ladies and gentlemen, I would like to introduce you to my son: the world's greatest drama king."

"Look who's talking." Davey playfully elbowed Joe.

"Be kind, you two," Ella chided.

"On with the story," Sammy said, slapping the table with a touch of amused impatience.

"Well, the point we're trying to make is that—"

"No, no," Joe said quickly, cutting Ella off. "Let's not skip to the end before the story has been told!"

"Then tell it, and stop using me as a drawing board to perfect your witty banter," Ella said.

"My banter does not need perfecting in order to be witty," Joe said, grinning. "I've just been setting the stage for the story to have its ultimate and re-sounding final meaning."

Ella raised an eyebrow. "Is the stage sufficiently set?"

"Indeed it is. Please continue, El Bell."

She nodded. "So, I tried to wake him, and even with the water he wouldn't budge. I got angry. Well, angrier."

"So...what did you do?"

Ella's cheeks turned a darker shade of pink and she shook her head. "Nothing. I was stubborn. I was angry. I had baked the pie for, I felt, no reason. Joe clearly wasn't grateful for the effort, and wasn't going to give me any effort of his own."

"Sleepy," Joe interjected. "I was sleepy—not un-grateful."

Ella gave him a look: raised her eyebrows, lowered the corners of her mouth...he knew the meaning.

"I know; I know...the only thing coming out of my mouth should be silence."

"And, by definition, that means we shouldn't hear it."

Joe chuckled. "Continue, my dear."

She shook her head and pursed her lips at his interruption, but began again. "So I did nothing more with the pie...and I forgot about it...in the oven."

"Oh no!"

"Oh yes," she said, a smile returning to her face. "Trust me, Davey, you never want to see—much less *smell*—something as black as that pie was. It smoked up the entire house."

Joe looked at Ella for permission to speak. She didn't grant it. He scrunched his lips and nose but remained silent, obedient. *I bet Mom is enjoying this.*

"It woke your dad up. But he is so sweet... he didn't complain about the smell, question why the house was smoky, or say a single negative thing. He could have made a comment about how I couldn't do something as simple as baking a pie and removing it *before* it turned to ash. All he said was, 'Well, looks like the pie is done.'

"Now, I should have laughed. He was trying to be cute and funny. But I stormed out of the house, ordered him to clean up the mess, and spent the rest of the day with Margaret."

Joe shook his head, forgetting his promise of silence. "That wasn't a fun mess to clean up, either. Even opening all the windows didn't get rid of all the smoke. By the time she came home, I was just as cranky as she was."

Ella nodded. "Yes, and that put me right back into the sour mood I had before Margaret calmed me down."

"So...lots of crankiness. I get it," Davey said. "Um...what are you trying to say?"

Ella gave Joe another look; a different one, which he still knew how to translate. "I told you we should have just said it outright," she said. "Parables have never worked for us, and you know it."

Joe smiled. "We're telling you that everyone has problems. Every couple fights. It's normal...and it's nothing to worry about. Your mom and I didn't talk without frustration in our voices for three days after The Great Pie Fiasco happened. Look at us now."

"Still arguing as always," Davey said, but smiled.

"And still terribly in love with each other, in spite of that," Ella said, interlacing her fingers with Joe's.

Davey nodded. "I've seen enough of your fights to know to expect them with Mical," he assured them. "But, well... What's happening with us now is a little deeper than a burnt pie."

"What *is* happening with you and Mical, Davey?" Ella wore her concerned face once again.

Joe sat at the table beside them, and they both waited for Davey to speak. He wanted to do it in a way that would point the least amount of blame at Mical. He couldn't change anything about Mical's actions, but he could change his reactions.

When we finally work things out, I don't want her past—our past—to have any effect on the way they see her.

Chapter 6

Mical put a hand on her stomach, wishing it could stop the pain. She needed another visit to the bathroom.

Anna looked up from her notebook. "You okay?" she mouthed.

Mical shrugged, but set her pen down. This couldn't wait. She stood, trying not to be noticed in the quiet room of test-taking students, and hurried into the hall.

She didn't return to class, but sat in the hall until the test was over. *Maybe I can make it up on a day I'm not sick.*

Anna brought both their things out, and smiled when she saw her. "I didn't think the test was *that* bad."

Mical took her backpack with a quiet word of thanks.

Anna watched her cautiously. "Well, you look a little better than you did earlier...what's up?"

"Just a bug, I guess." She shrugged. "It's probably the flu. Everyone seems to be getting that."

"That makes sense," Anna said. "Sorry, Mically. Being sick isn't fun."

She shrugged. "Everyone gets it." *This is different than the flu, though.*

"Are you hungry?"

Mical nodded. Her breakfast had left her stomach hours before.

"Good." She started walking outside, motioning for Mical to follow. "You can join Peyton and me for lunch."

"You're going to lunch with Peyton?" Mical couldn't keep the surprise out of her voice, and the last word came out higher than she'd intended.

"Someone needs to keep that boy in line." Anna laughed as she pushed the school's door open. "You can help."

They found a table in McDonald's just as Peyton entered. He grinned at them.

I wish Davey would greet me like that.

Anna waved him over. "We got you a Big Mac. Figured that was safe."

"Sounds awesome." He dug a twenty out of his pocket.

She shook her head as she pushed her backpack to the ground to give him a place to sit. "It's fine. You can pay next time."

"I'll hold you to that," he sat by her with a smile.

Mical watched them for a moment, disinterestedly curious—if that was possible. She faintly heard a number called and checked the receipt. *I think that's ours.* She retrieved their food from the counter and thanked the attendant.

Peyton took the tray from her and placed it in the center of the table. "How was the test?"

"You mean the one you were supposed to be at?" Anna shook her head.

He shrugged. "The prof. is an easy grader. I'm not worried." He sneaked a french fry.

Anna playfully slapped his hand. "It's pretty easy to give an F to a test that wasn't finished; I agree."

Mical frowned as she picked up her hamburger.

Anna glanced at her apologetically. "It would be different if there was a good reason for it."

"Sleep is always a good reason," Peyton countered and opened the box of his Big Mac.

Mical unwrapped her burger and took a bite. The smell nearly overwhelmed her, and she felt her stomach growing queasy again.

Anna took her chicken sandwich off the tray. "If you want more than the small size of fries, you're getting them yourself. They don't sound good to me and Mical today."

Peyton shrugged. "I'm good with this," he said, motioning to his burger.

Mical stood up. "I'll be right back," she mumbled.

"...Was it something I said?" she heard Peyton ask as she headed for the bathroom.

McDonald's kept their heat on low, or possibly had never turned their AC off. Summer had ended a couple months earlier, but she was grateful for the temperature. Warmth would have been worse.

Mical joined them at the table again a few minutes later. Anna watched her curiously. "Maybe you should go lie down," she suggested.

"Do I look that bad?" Mical almost smiled.

She shrugged. "I just think you could use some rest."

"What do you think will be on Professor Scott's final?" Mical asked, turning to Peyton to avoid Anna's watchful eyes.

He shrugged.

"Are you actually going to show up to that one?" Anna asked.

"Depends what my other options are," Peyton smirked.

"You can't slide by in college, Pey," Anna set her chicken down. "You don't need straight A's, but you do need to *pass*."

He shrugged again. "Don't worry about it, AnnaBear. Teachers love me."

"Brown-nosing the teacher will only get you so far," Mical said, grateful the focus had shifted away from her.

"Who said anything about brown-nosing? It's just my natural charm." He grinned, as if to prove it.

Mical rolled her eyes, but Anna giggled. She offered a look of betrayal that Anna conveniently failed to notice.

Mical felt her stomach tense up again as she tried to take another bite of her burger. She set her food down in frustration. "I guess I do need to rest," she said. "I'm going home."

"Do you want a ride?" Anna asked, putting her half-eaten food on the tray and gathering her things.

Mical shook her head. "I'm used to riding the bus. Thanks." She headed outside before Anna had a chance to hug her goodbye. The cold Minnesota air greeted her as she exited the McDonald's. *I wonder why my stomach is being so weird.* At least now she was too cold for it to have much of an effect on her. *Small comfort that is, though.*

Davey had only been gone a day, and already she missed him. *Isn't this when husbands are supposed to be around? When you just want to curl up and cry, they understand, and hold you until you feel better.* She sighed and rubbed her arm as she waited for the bus to arrive.

Or maybe that's just what Hollywood likes to pretend it's like. After marrying Davey, I don't believe any of those lies.

Besides, she didn't deserve that kind of treatment.

I'm as worthless as my father says I am.

She climbed onto the bus, nodded acknowledgement at the driver, and sat hunched over in the first open seat. She held her stomach in a futile attempt to calm the pain.

A moment later, there was a gentle touch on her shoulder. She looked up slightly and saw a wrinkled hand resting there.

"When is he coming?" the elderly lady asked.

Mical shrugged, and wondered why the family of this senile grandmother hadn't put her in a nursing home yet.

"Have you named him, yet?" she asked, undeterred.

She won't leave unless you answer. "Sure," Mical said, not even trying to keep the annoyance out of her voice. "Chair. I named it chair."

A look of confusion crossed the lady's face. "That's...an interesting name for a baby." She shrugged and turned to find a seat farther in the bus.

As the strange woman walked away, Michal heard her mumble, "Parents these days think they can name their children any old thing. It ain't right."

Crazy old woman, Mical thought, and hunched over once again.

She exited at the stop near her house and walked the rest of the way.

The two-bedroom cottage was quiet without Davey there. She turned on all the lights and got a can of Sprite from the fridge. The can cooled her forehead, and she trudged to the couch to lie down.

Davey's phone sat undisturbed on the coffee table, where she'd left it after she put it back together the day before. Mical picked it up with her free hand and turned it on.

Her own face, caught unaware but smiling, greeted her as the background image. Happy, lonely, tears came to her eyes.

I shouldn't, she thought, but still clicked the "Messages" icon. A list of names popped up: Mom, Mically, Dad, Jonathan, and Robbieboy.

She didn't have to tap her name to know what was in that thread: boring tidbits from her about study sessions, Davey apologizing for working overtime, and both wondering when the other wanted to eat.

Mical touched the screen over the "Mom" thread and started reading the most recent texts.

Mom: I love you, Davey
Davey: I love you too
Mom: We miss you. I thought we would see you more.
Davey: I'm sorry. I'll try to visit soon.
Mom: Bring your beautiful Mical, too.
Davey: Of course.
Mom: Good

Mical wondered what it would be like to have a mom to text. The little she remembered of her own mother wasn't enough to help her imagination.

She felt her stomach tense again. She sighed, then backed out of the thread. Onto "Robbieboy."

I think that's his brother...

Davey: Hey turdface
Robbieboy: Hey bucketnose

Mical laughed in spite of the pain she was feeling.

Davey: How's your girl?
Robbieboy: Frustrating + wonderful
Davey: Haha
Robbieboy: Yours?
Davey: She's great

Really?

Robbieboy: So you're still head over heels for her
Davey: No

Mical swallowed, trying to keep tears away. It wasn't fair of her to expect feelings to remain when they were based on a lie.

She almost turned off the phone, but curiosity—and perhaps a little self-loathing—told her to keep reading.

Davey: I never was
Robbieboy: Oh, that's right. You didn't fall, you "chose" to love
Davey: Still do. Every day.

Well, that's about as unromantic as it gets. She hadn't made a "choice" to love him; it just happened. *That's how love works.*

Yet...when Davey was around, even with the deception and everything, she never had questioned his feelings for her.

Maybe I should have.

At least she knew he wasn't completely giving up. Romantic or not, he was making a daily choice to love her. She turned the phone off and put it back in the bedroom.

He wouldn't be so nosy if our situations were switched.

Her stomach calmed enough after a few hours that she began to feel hungry.

She started searching the fridge, and eventually settled on pickles, an orange, and peanut butter. She dropped them together in a bowl and mixed, then ate the whole thing. The combination almost didn't seem strange to her.

She woke the next morning with renewed stomach pains, and no desire to go to class. After unsuccessfully keeping neither breakfast nor supper the night before inside, she decided it could be more than the flu.

She rubbed her hands together as she waited for the bus yet again; a new purpose this time.

The bus driver nodded as she presented her pass to her, and she moved to the back.

The trip to the doctor felt long compared to the short ride to her school.

She arrived in time for the appointment she had made. After waiting fifteen minutes in the patient-filled lobby, a nurse brought her to an empty, sterile room and gave her a cup for a urine test, which she handed back a few moments later. The nurse promised the doctor would be with her shortly.

In medical language, "shortly" is "approximately an hour." The doctor found her with her head in her hands, leaning as far over the examining table as she dared.

She explained as concisely as she could. The doctor nodded as she examined the results of the urine HCG test. "Hmm..." Dr. Dore said, revealing nothing.

Mical was in too much pain to question it.

The doctor began to perform a physical exam, checking Mical's heart rate with a stethoscope and palpating her abdomen.

Mical winced at the touch.

Dr. Dore moved the stethoscope to Mical's stomach.

She jumped slightly. "What...what are you doing?"

"Listening for a heartbeat," Dr. Dore said in a matter-of-fact tone.

"My heart's higher..."

The doctor held a finger to her lips, and Mical quieted.

"I'm calling for a bedside ultrasound."

Mical stared at her. "Like...for a baby?"

"Exactly."

"I'm not pregnant," Mical said, moving to the edge of the table.

"All the symptoms say you are."

Mical shook her head. "No," she insisted. "It's not possible."

The doctor frowned. "I understand if you don't want it. There are other options—adoption, abortion—"

"No," Mical said again. "I would welcome it if it was possible. I can't have children. My body isn't capable of it." *You're a doctor; you should know this.*

She'd known since she was fifteen—maybe even before. Many tears were cried over it, but she'd finally come to accept it. How dare this doctor give her false hope?

The doctor shrugged as a nurse brought in the machine. "If it isn't pregnancy, perhaps this will show us what it really is."

The nurse prepared Mical's stomach for the ultrasound. The cool gel soothed her stomach, so Mical didn't protest.

She leaned back and let the doctor watch the screen. She didn't know what she'd find, but she didn't want to see it.

"Mrs. Blake...look," the doctor's voice held restrained joy.

Mical reluctantly turned to the screen, and saw several little blobs.

Dr. Dore pointed to a lighter area, still smiling. "There's your baby."

...Baby? It can't be.

"Congratulations, Mrs. Blake," the nurse smiled.

There must be some other explanation. This makes no sense.

The nurse cleaned Mical's stomach as the doctor wrote a list of what she could expect in the coming months, and gave an approximation of her due date. She began collecting pamphlets of pregnancy dos and don'ts.

Maybe I should get a second opinion.

The Dr. Dore sent Mical home with a pile of papers, and recommended some classes for her and her husband, to help them prepare.

Mical left the office in silence, gripping tightly to the papers.

Chapter 7

Mical hadn't grown up the way he had. He'd never met her mother, but it was difficult not to judge somebody who put their children into the control of someone as cruel as her father.

God did say to love your enemies and honor your father. In a sense, Simon Benson was both. But it was difficult.

How can I love someone who has so intentionally hurt the woman I hold most dear?

Ella stood and kissed his forehead, motioned for Joe to follow, and they moved to the stove. There was nothing left there but an empty pot, but she knew it would be easier for him if his audience wasn't staring directly at him.

As an excuse, Joe found a bag of salad in the fridge and started a hunt for other vegetables to add to it.

Davey picked up his fork and moved the noodles around on the plate, still unable to put his situation into words.

I'm here because Mical is paranoid. But the issues in our situation are deeper than just that.

He had taken her from her father when they had married. That was Davey's way of protecting her.

Mr. Benson could abuse her when she lived with him. In his mind, that gave him power over her. He had no control now; no way to hurt her...except through Davey.

No. She's being unreasonable about that.

Mical was no longer a helpless child. Her father's words could no longer hurt her...could they? *Can mine?*

He couldn't change her childhood, but he could still be certain that her present and future were far better.

"How long did your honeymoon phase last?" he asked as he twirled his sauce-covered spaghetti.

Ella bit her lip and stayed silent, allowing Joe to answer.

His answer was as helpful as her silence. "I don't know, exactly...a month or two, I suppose. It's different for everyone, though, Davey. You can't compare marriages."

"Okay," he said, "but...one more question. Did the honeymoon period start right away?"

"Of course," Ella said, frowning slightly. "Why are you asking?"

He let out a low breath. "Because, either our honeymoon stage hasn't started yet, or it lasted only two days."

Ella returned to making the plates of salad, and Joe started peeling and cutting up cucumbers to put on top.

"Well," Joe said hesitantly, "I did tell you it was different for everybody, didn't I?"

Ella scowled. "That is *not* what he needs to hear right now, Joe. Sweetie," she turned to Davey again, "you do know that the honeymoon period does not mean free of fights, right?"

Davey nodded, and then let out another low breath. "Honestly," he said, "fights would be far easier to handle; far easier to fix. I don't know if there is even a name for whatever it is that's happening with Mical and I. We just...we're not happy."

Ella nodded, urging him in her gentle way to continue.

"Before we married, I *was* happy and content. Not perfectly so, but who is? I wasn't expecting marriage to fix everything. But I also wasn't expecting it to...take that happiness away." He winced at his words; they hadn't come out as he had intended. "That is—*I've* been making Mical unhappy, and not being able to change that is making *me* unhappy." He frowned. "I mean, we do fight some."

"What are the fights about?" Joe asked.

Davey considered. *A lot of things...* "Mical wants me to stop working for her father. She thinks I've given him power over me. But with Papa, no one can have that kind of power."

"And she is having a difficult time understanding that?" Joe asked.

He nodded. "She has a difficult time understanding anything that has to do with God," he said truthfully.

"Well, she is still very new to it all," Ella offered. *I wish that was all it was.*

"You already know where the problem lies, don't you, Davey," Ella said. It wasn't a question.

Yes, I do. He stabbed at a noodle and missed. They had to be told. "Mical isn't a Christian," he said quietly.

Joe's knife slipped, and he made a slight grunt of pain as it nicked his unprotected skin. "Ow," he said weakly.

Ella glanced at the wound, but apparently decided it wasn't bad enough to need attention. Joe disappeared in the direction of the bathroom.

"How long have you known?" Ella asked gently.

Davey shrugged and made another unsuccessful stab.

"You know," Joe said, "you could have led into that more—given some kind of warning. You could have started the sentence with a 'well,' even. Or at the very least," he said, chuckling a little and motioning to his now-bandaged hand, "you could have waited to tell us until I no longer had a dangerous weapon in my possession."

"That little thing is considered a dangerous weapon?" Davey shook his head at the small knife Joe had been using for the cucumbers.

"The definition of a dangerous weapon," Joe said, "is something that causes harm. That knife has caused me harm."

"And exactly whose definition are you working under, Dad?"

"Exactly my own," he said with a pleased grin.

"That's what I thought," Davey said.

Ella shook her head at them. "How long have you known, Davey?" she asked again. Anticipating a witty response from Joe, she clarified: "How long have you known that Mical wasn't a Christian?"

Davey frowned. "I guess I always had suspicions. I told myself they were unfounded. At least at first, she did seem sincere."

"When was the last time you prayed?" Ella asked. "I mean, about this."

Davey thought about it, and came up empty. "I don't know…"

"Then why don't we start there?" Joe suggested. "Let's pray for guidance."

Ella and Joe joined Davey and Sammy at the table.

There was a moment of silence when the prayer ended.

"Well," Davey said slowly, "I still don't feel guided."

Joe smiled. "I guess God isn't giving out the instant stuff today."

Davey smiled a little, too. "Yeah, I guess He reserves that for Tuesdays and Thursdays."

"Oh, naturally. Just pray again when Tuesday comes around, and you'll get it."

Ella playfully shoved Joe's arm. "Come on, Joe. Knock it off."

"*Me* knock it off? You are the one abusing people for no good reason!"

"Believe me, I had a reason." She stood and set the plates of salad on the table.

"Yes, but was it a good one?"

"I'm forming an even better one as we speak."

"Point taken," Joe said.

The room grew quiet.

"What do *you* think I should I do?" Davey asked. "What would you do if you were in my position? I love Mical…it's just…"

Ella nodded understandingly as she sat down. "It's hard, when you feel that what you centered your marriage around is no longer at the center; perhaps never was."

Davey nodded, surprised at how well her words described his feelings.

She continued, "And maybe that was the case for Mical…but it isn't the case for you, Davey."

He nodded again, remembering the countless prayers he had uttered on Mical's behalf, even before feelings had begun to form. That number had only increased when he realized he was falling for her.

"You see, Davey, God is there, right where you want Him to be," Ella said, pouring Italian dressing on her lettuce. "Mical may not realize it, and some-times—probably quite often—it may be difficult for even you to see. But He *is* there."

"He is the One who goes with you. He will not leave you nor forsake you," Joe quoted. "You are His child. I always loved that verse."

"God is so much bigger than unspoken pray-ers," Ella said.

"Yes," Joe said, moving his salad around the plate. "And He is so much bigger than one person's skepticism."

Davey nodded. The words didn't bring the peace he was hoping for, but they were somehow comfort-ing. They assured him he was doing all that he was able to.

"God brings people into our lives for a reason," Joe said, preparing an extra-large bite. "He brought you and Mical together for a reason." He got a mis-chievous glint in his eye as he continued. "Going as far as marrying her to discover what that reason was may have been a little much, but..." He grinned and took a bite.

"Joe." Ella gave him a stern warning look.

Joe quickly chewed and swallowed. "*But,*" he said, "since you were led to do so, He is going to use your marriage. It may be very soon, and may not be not for many years. Just wait."

"And the world is full of rainbows and daisies, even in the winter months," Davey said with a sar-castic smile. "I had almost forgotten about your never-ending optimism."

"There are some parts of the world that still have rainbows and daisies when it's winter for you and me."

Ella cleared her throat.

Joe nodded. "I completely agree, Ella."

Davey wondered if he and Mical would *ever* be as close as his parents. *Not unless things really start to change.* He twirled noodles around his fork.

"Davey, as usual, you have completely skipped over my point."

"I get your point," he said. "God can use anything. It's just that...it *is* hard to deal with...so the fact that someday, somewhere, sometime, some good may finally come out of it... Well, Dad, that isn't very comforting right now."

Joe nodded.

The timer began its annoying stream of beeps, and Joe hurried to free the garlic bread from the warm prison of the oven.

Ella and Joe returned home a few days later, and Davey had some cherished alone time with a man he had admired for years.

Sammy woke each morning promptly at five, and waited patiently with his tea until Davey trudged out of bed between seven and eight.

He greeted Davey with a grin, and only a touch of a "'bout time you woke up" attitude. Sammy offered tea, and Davey made coffee; he fed them both sausage-dotted eggs as they silently watched squirrels and birds.

It was a comforting routine, and if it had only included Mical, Davey would have been completely content.

In her absence, it didn't even matter that she didn't believe what he did.

Of course, he knew he was fooling himself. It would always matter. But with his parents' and Sammy's help, he was learning how to handle it when things returned to 'normal.'

Sammy turned his attention from a squirrel trying to steal a metal acorn from a lawn ornament and watched Davey for a moment. "Thinking about your darling again, eh?"

Davey smiled. "All the time."

He nodded in understanding. "Papa will tell you when the time is right."

"I'm counting on it," Davey agreed with a smile.

"David," Sammy said.

Davey's smile faded in response to Sammy's tone.

"I don't often ask for favors I can't repay," he began, his voice steady and deliberate.

Davey nodded. "Anything, Sammy," he promised.

"My sweet niece married last fall, and no one has heard from her lately. It's unlike her to disappear." He handed Davey a wrinkled letter he had been grasping. "She sent me this today."

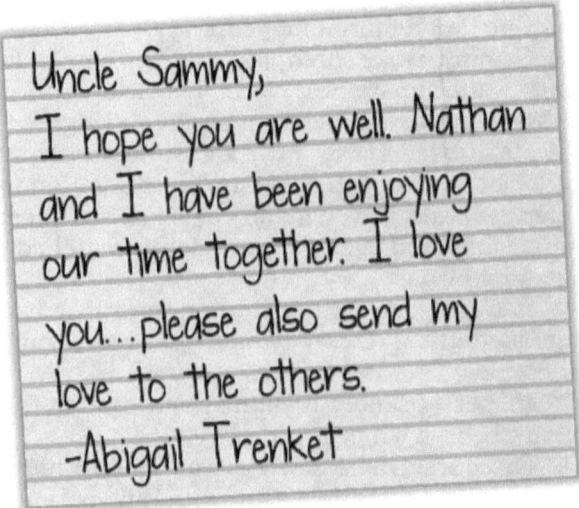

Uncle Sammy,
I hope you are well. Nathan and I have been enjoying our time together. I love you...please also send my love to the others.
-Abigail Trenket

Davey read it, though the meaning wasn't clear to him.

"All is not well, David. I would go myself if I could, but as it is, I must ask this of you instead.

Please, David, find Abigail and be certain she is safe. Take care of her for me."

Davey nodded.

Sammy handed him the envelope, which had a town in Wisconsin listed, but not a full address. "Please go soon,"

"Today," Davey promised. He gathered their dishes before beginning to pack his things. "Will you be okay on your own?"

Sammy smiled. "I'm never alone," he reminded him. He picked up his mug of tea. "Now get out of here."

Davey nodded, and swung his bag over his shoulder.

"Thank you, son," Sammy said. "If God had blessed me with children, He couldn't have given me better than you."

Davey chuckled. "I'm sure He could have, Sammy...but thank you." He hugged Sammy.

"Take some coffee with you, Davey," Sammy said. "Consider that my parting advice. Always bring coffee on a long drive."

Davey chuckled and filled a Styrofoam cup.

A few hours later, Davey drove into Diamond Bluff, Wisconsin. No one had heard of Abigail, at least not the one he was likely talking about, and only a couple recognized—but couldn't place—the name Nathan. The small town had a feel similar to Backus. If Abigail lived there, everyone would have known.

She was trying to hide her location. But why put anything in the return address?

The grocery clerk directed him to the home of a reserved, somewhat mysterious couple on the town's border. "Might be them," he said. "I hope you find who you're looking for." He smiled as Davey bought a pack of gum he didn't really need.

Davey thanked him and drove in the direction the clerk had pointed. A white house with peeling paint and half the shutters missing came into view.

It looked empty, but for the dim glow of a candle through one of the basement windows.

He knocked on the door. Perhaps the information he had been given was false. If Sammy's niece was okay, he could head home to Mical. *I miss her.*

A thin young woman opened the door just a crack.

"Abigail?"

She nearly closed it, but Davey blocked it with his fingers, grimacing with the pain. "Is that your name?" he asked when he could find words again.

"You shouldn't be here," she said.

"Please, Abigail, I need to know."

"Who are you?" her voice was stronger, but not demanding. She kept the door almost closed.

"I'm a friend of your uncle—Sammy. My name is Davey."

Abigail dropped the door, letting it swing open slightly. "How is Uncle Sammy?" she asked, her voice trembling.

Davey smiled. "As wonderful as always—but he's worried about you. How shall I tell him you are doing?"

She let out a laugh, unguardedly joyful. Davey couldn't help but smile in response. "Same as what I said in the letter. Dear Uncle Sammy never did trust the postal service."

Davey chuckled, glad to see Sammy's fears were unfounded.

Abigail looked beyond Davey before opening the door completely. "Please come in. Tell me what you can about my favorite uncle—and about yourself." She made him a mug of tea and sat across from him at the round kitchen table.

He told her what he could about Sammy, and she smiled in response.

"Oh, how I miss that man." She let out a soft sigh as she lifted her mug, but her smile remained unwavering.

"I'm sure he would love a visit," Davey offered.

She nodded without making any promises. "Are you hungry?" She didn't wait for a response before pulling several Tupperware containers from the fridge. She piled a plate high with food and put it in the microwave.

Davey chuckled.

"Now... How do you know my uncle?"

Davey could still remember the first time he had met Sammy. He had been grudgingly helping his mom in the garden when Sammy came and asked him for a tomato. Davey had shrugged and picked a green one, then watched in awe as Sammy tended it so it would continue to ripen, and picked a red one instead. He explained the importance of letting things wait until it was their time; a lesson Davey had never forgotten—though he hadn't always followed it.

"We were neighbors when I was about ten years old. He moved to his place 'in the country' a couple years later, but we kept in touch. He's been a wonderful mentor for me."

Abigail's relentless smile grew. "He's been my mentor, too—no matter how far or close we've been to each other. He's a good man."

Davey nodded.

Abigail put the steaming food in front of him, and gave him silence for a moment as he took a bite of the potatoes.

"I'm glad you came," she said, resting her chin in her hands as she watched him eat. "It's so nice to hear what Uncle Sammy has been up to."

Davey chuckled. "He would have told you himself if you'd given him an address to write to."

Abigail opened her mouth, but quickly closed it as something from the window behind him drew her attention. "Well, it was really nice to meet you," she said, standing. "Would you like me to box that up for you?" She motioned to his plate.

Davey stood, too, sensing her urgency. "That's all right—but it was very good. Thank you." He moved toward the door.

Abigail drew him into a hug. "Thank you for coming and talking with me."

Davey smiled. "Any time."

She closed and locked the door behind him. He turned in time to see the garage door close. *I wonder why she didn't want me to meet her husband.* He started walking back to his truck, but made it only halfway down the sidewalk before hearing yelling from an open window.

"Why are you lying to me?" the man's voice demanded, using an unsavory term for Abigail. "Was that another of your boyfriends?"

"No!" Abigail squeaked. "Nathan—please—the baby!"

There was a loud crash, then nothing.

Chapter 8

Mical arranged the nativity scene Chrissy had given her at her wedding—one of the few decorations she had for the upcoming holiday. Thanksgiving had passed without much notice from her, except to wonder how Davey was spending it. She'd taken the break as a chance to get ahead on school and prepare for her finals.

She placed Mary next to the manger and smiled a little at the figure of the baby. She felt her own stomach. If she focused, sometimes she imagined she could feel a tiny movement.

She glanced at the unopened mail on the table, already knowing what it would include.

Guess I need to do another sympathy-driven plea.

The first letter was from her school, reminding her to purchase books before the spring semester began. The next was from her bank, reminding her she had no money to buy them with. *At least that will change after Friday.*

The remaining mail consisted of past-due credit card statements, an energy bill, and a warning that without a speedy payment her phone would be shut off.

She piled them in order of importance and called her cell phone provider.

"My husband lost his job, I'm in school full time and just got a job, and we're expecting a baby," was her repeated explanation. "Please—is there anything you can do?"

She hated to beg, but it seemed her only option.

A few phone calls later had given her another month to pay the past due notices.

Working Christmas Day will help, she thought, to ease her nerves. She hadn't planned to celebrate the made-up holiday anyway.

Mical glanced at the clock.

Ten minutes.

She grabbed her purse and walked to the gas station two blocks away. She greeted the cashier without really looking at him, until he turned quickly to hide his face.

"...Peyton?"

His confidence returned, and he gave his usual grin. "Hey, Mickey."

"You work here too?"

He shrugged. "It passes the time."

She could think of many more pleasant things that would accomplish the same.

"Wait...too?"

She nodded. "I started last week." *I had no other choice once the bills really began to pile up.*

"Oh." He paused for a moment, arranging some candy around the counter before looking up and smiling at her. "Sweet!"

She shrugged, stepping behind the counter and finding her nametag in the drawer. "You seriously didn't notice this? How many people do you know named Mical?" She put it on.

Peyton shrugged. "I don't look in the drawers unless there's something I need." He looked at the clock. "Guess my shift is over. See you later, Mickey." He pinned his tag to the corkboard.

"Um..." she looked at the little store around her, and focused on the cash register. *How am I supposed to use that? I was only taught to keep shelves stocked when I was here last.* "I wasn't really trained to run the store alone yet."

His shoulders lowered. "Just play cashier with the customers and keep the shelves stocked," he said with a shake of his head. "There are extras of pretty much everything in the back. Make a note if something needs to be reordered, and if there are problems, the manager's number is taped to the counter." Peyton grabbed his bag and walked to the door.

Mical stared at the counter, feeling lost. Customers wandered the shop, and soon they would need her help. *What if I mess up?*

A gust of cold air joined her as Peyton opened the door. He glanced at her and raised his hand in a wave, but frowned when he saw her face. "Okay, Mical," he closed the door and returned to the counter. "I guess I've got nothing better to do today. You can act like I'm not here, but if you need something tell me."

He dragged a chair across the floor and pulled a book from his bag. Using a shelf behind the counter as a footstool, he leaned back in the chair and started to read. "Pay attention," he said.

Mical turned when someone began placing items on the counter. She glanced at Peyton.

"Be friendly," he mouthed.

Mical gave a nervous smile and greeted the woman.

She nodded and held up her credit card.

Mical picked up the items and, after some searching, found the barcodes. She placed them over the red laser one at a time, and hoped the beeps meant she was doing it right.

The woman glanced at her phone and waved the card.

"Is there gas with this?" Mical asked, glancing at Peyton for a nod of approval.

The woman said no, and shook her card in Mical's direction again. Mical took it for a moment, but didn't see a way to enter the number. She saw a card reader by the woman's elbow.

"Um...please slide it there," she said, handing the card back.

With a sigh of impatience, the woman swiped her card. Mical handed her the receipt without a word.

"Be grateful," Peyton said in a voice only she could hear.

"Thank you," Mical said with another forced smile. "Have a nice day."

The woman said nothing as she gathered her things and left the store.

"Decent job," Peyton said. "Next time try not to be so unnatural."

Mical rubbed her arm. "I'd never used the cash register before. Give me a break."

"That's fair, but you still don't have to grit your teeth at the customers." He chuckled.

"Most people call that a smile," she said, demonstrating.

"Nobody calls *that* a smile."

She shrugged.

"I'll start telling jokes back here if I need to. And, trust me; you don't want to hear my jokes."

Mical smiled, more genuinely this time.

Peyton grinned. "That's more like it."

Her grin turned to a grimace as her baby reminded her he was there. She gripped her stomach instinctively.

"...Mical?"

She forced her back to straighten, moved her hand to the counter, and pasted on a smile once more.

"When are you due?" Peyton closed his book and watched her.

"What?"

"I have younger siblings. I know that pose."

She sighed. "Not for months. Like, June."

He nodded. "That will come quick, if my mother is to be believed."

"And what is your perspective?"

He shrugged. "It doesn't affect *me* all that much, so I'm not the one to ask. Time passes as it always does...and then there's a cute little baby at the end." He smiled.

She nodded. *Can I really have a little one?* It still seemed too good to be real.

Peyton shrugged and set his book under the counter. "If you need a break, let me know."

"I'm not an invalid. I can do my job." She glanced at his book; it was an advanced math. "Are you taking that class this spring?"

He shook his head.

"Then...why?"

"Can't a guy like math?" he smirked.

She picked up the book and flipped it open. "You actually understand this?"

"Nah, I just like looking at the pictures." Peyton grinned. "Of course I understand it."

"Okay, what does this one mean?" she pointed to a symbol in the book.

He looked over her shoulder and where her finger was resting. "That's the symbol for division. I'm surprised you didn't learn that one...in elementary school."

"Not *that* one," she closed the book and hit him with it.

He chuckled. "I mean it, though—about taking a break. Everyone needs one sometimes. I've seen enough of my mom's pregnancy tantrums to know the importance of break time for you people." He winked.

"What is that supposed to mean?"

"You're caring for a little one. You've gotta not...overexert yourself."

She rolled her eyes, but said, "Okay," with a sigh. "Thanks, I guess."

He shrugged and retrieved his book from where Mical had placed it on the counter.

Another customer was waiting to pay, and Mical could feel her heartbeat increase as she prepared to serve them. Her hands shook as she scanned the first item. "Cash or credit?" she asked, hoping for credit.

The customer held up a $10. "No gas today."

She nodded and took the money. She looked at the register for a moment. *Now what?*

Peyton reached around her and hit a button that said "Cash". The drawer popped open and hit her, gently, in the stomach.

She put the money in and counted the change.

"Can I have a receipt?"

"Of course," she forced a smile. *But...how?*

Peyton stood and typed the amount of cash into the machine, and it printed a receipt with the change amount due. He handed both to the customer, as well as a free pack of gum as an apology for the delay.

Mical grew more confident as she served more customers and no longer needed Peyton to step in.

The store grew quiet again, with only one person outside at a pump.

Mical turned to Peyton, who seemed enthralled by his textbook. "How many siblings do you have?" she asked.

"Too many," he mumbled, turning the page. His forehead creased and he flipped back to the previous page.

"That's probably a different number for everyone."

"No, math isn't subjective like most subjects. That's why I like it."

She blinked. "I meant the number of siblings…"

He shrugged. "How many do *you* have?" he asked.

"Two."

"I have more than that."

"How many more?" she asked; her lips began curling upward.

He shrugged. "Three full, one step, and two half—that I know of. Don't know how many halves there are running around."

"Oh," she said. Her smile lessened.

"Yep. Not everyone has the perfect little family you do."

Mical blinked. *What?* "Perfect?" She nearly laughed.

"Sure. You're daddy's little girl; mommy's princess; and Davey's queen." He shrugged. "That seems pretty perfect to me."

"Yeah, if it was really like that, it would be."

He lowered his chin. "Don't tell me the baby isn't Davey's."

She slapped him, and he nearly lost his balance. "Sorry," he mumbled, regaining his nonchalance. "No need to be so touchy. People have affairs. It happens."

"Not me," she said, wanting to hit him again.

"Okay. I'm sorry. I shouldn't have said that." He almost sounded sincere.

She shrugged, and went around the counter to start making a list of items to restock.

He joined her a moment later. "I really am sorry, Mical. I was joking—but I forgot you're a Christian and that kind of thing offends you."

"I'm not—" she began, but finished with "—offended."

"Oh, you just slapped me for fun. I see." Peyton chuckled.

She sighed. "Sure."

"Good to know, I suppose. Next time your hand starts moving I'll remember to duck."

She counted the boxes of Skittles left on the shelf and made a note to bring out four more.

Peyton shrugged and returned to his book.

Mical completed the list, approved the customer at the pump when he was ready, and started restocking the shelves.

Peyton jumped up and brought out the heavier boxes before she had a chance to. "What did I tell you about overexertion? It's no good for babies."

Her eyes moved to the ceiling in annoyance, but she secretly appreciated his help. "Is it usually this quiet here?"

He glanced up from a box he'd been cutting open. "Hmm?"

"Are there ever more customers?" she asked.

"Sometimes," he said. "Most people pay at the pump unless they need the bathroom or have a weird craving for gas station snacks." He pulled the bottles of juice from the box and added them to the shelf. "It gets pretty busy on the weekends and around five, when people are on their way home from work. Besides that," he shrugged, "it's pretty quiet. Bring books. The manager does it, too. If it doesn't affect how you work, no one cares."

"Okay," she said, making a mental note to bring her schoolbooks once she got them. *Maybe I can find used ones.* "What classes are you taking next semester?" she asked.

Peyton's expression seemed to change slightly, though she may have imagined the lowering of his lips and the tiny crease in his brow. He shrugged.

"You don't know?"

"Not officially," he said. "I might end up just quitting."

She stared at him for a moment, before telling herself that it was just another of his jokes. She laughed. "Good one."

His serious expression didn't budge. "It's not a joke, Mical."

"You can't quit. Isn't your graduation like...one year from now?"

"It's in two years, actually—and a semester be-cause I didn't plan well and took classes I didn't need at first."

"Close enough, Peyton. Suck it up and power through it."

He shrugged again.

"Sometimes I don't understand you. Not every-one can treat money as lightly as you do, and no one should. If you can afford college, it's irrespon-sible to waste two years of it and just drop out."

"That's great, coming from the girl whose daddy pays for everything." Peyton rolled his eyes.

She narrowed hers. "My father pays for *noth-ing*," she said, slamming boxes of crackers on the empty shelf. "He hasn't for a long time."

"Aw, did you make him angry?"

"Just shut up. You're too pea-brained to under-stand. Is that why you're quitting?" She smirked. "Is the reason you miss classes and tests because you know you'll get an F either way?"

"I'm quitting because I don't have thousands of dollars to spend on it—this crappy job doesn't give me enough to cover even just one semester—and I wasn't one of the lucky few who was given a scholarship. If I skip class, it means I had to work. I couldn't switch shifts even though, believe me, I tried, and I couldn't afford to forgo the pay."

Mical frowned. "I thought you were here just to pass the time."

"I'm not, okay? No one would take a job like this 'for fun'."

She nodded, slowly. "I'm sorry. I thought…"

"I know. I learned how to fit in around the richer areas. You don't make friends if everyone knows you as the janitor's son. So I compensated, and it became a habit."

"You don't have to act with me," she said, her tone gentle with sympathy. "I've been on both sides of the financial ladder. It doesn't change who I am either way."

He nodded. "Anna doesn't like the act, either."

"She knows?"

"She has for a while. We grew up together."

Mical wondered what else she didn't know about her friends. *I guess I've never taken the time to learn these kinds of things,* she thought, disappointed at her self-centered nature.

Yet I've expected them to want to learn what was happening with me. Anna, at least. She made another internal vow to improve.

Chapter 9

Davey ran back to the house. He knew the door was locked, so he searched instead for the open window. He found it along the side of the house, and was glad to see it was large enough for him. It was placed about four feet from the ground—a difficult but not impossible height. He pushed it open enough to climb through, scrambled inside, and landed with a thud. He quickly stood, allowing himself only a moment to wince from the pain of his fall.

Abigail, where are you?

As he exited the bathroom and came into the living room, he found her husband instead.

"Who are you?" The man, who had heard Davey's entrance, swung a bat dangerously close to his head.

"A friend," Davey said, ducking and holding up his hands to calm the man.

Nathan cursed in disbelief. "Who are you really? Come to steal from us?" He swung the bat again.

Davey stepped back but scanned the room for Abigail. "Where is she?"

"Now it comes out. Oh, Abby, the lover you claimed you didn't have is here. Won't you come out and say hi?"

Davey let out a breath of relief as Abigail emerged, trembling but safe, from one of the bedrooms. His concern grew once more as he saw the swelling just starting to form around her eyes.

"Why don't you tell your boyfriend to run along home now, Abby?"

Abigail looked at the ground, holding the handle of the door for support.

"Speak up, Abby, we can't hear you."

She kept her eyes on the worn carpet below her. "You can go," she said to Davey, barely audible.

Davey frowned. "Nathan—that is your name, right?—if you lay another hand on her, you will regret it."

"Ooh, big words from a little boy," Nathan said.

Davey grabbed the collar of Nathan's shirt and held tight, not choking him, but proving his ability to. "Respect your wife or you will lose her," he said, his voice filled with semi-restrained anger.

"Get out of my house," Nathan growled, easily pushing him away.

Davey wasn't intimidated, but he didn't want to make things worse for his new friend. He turned to Abigail.

"Please," she said, "just go."

He nodded, and returned his attention to her husband. "I will do whatever it takes to protect Abigail," he said levelly, calm but dangerous. "Anything."

The man's expression didn't change.

"I'll know if you touch her again," Davey said, then exited the house.

He returned to his truck, praying he had done the right thing, and asked what his next step should be.

Clarity didn't come, but he knew he couldn't leave Abigail in the hands of this man.

The town had no hotel, and Davey didn't want to be too far from Abigail's home if she needed help again. Still, he knew staying would make things worse. He drove to the next street and pulled his winter coat from the back as he prepared to spend the night in his truck.

Davey awoke to a light tapping noise. He pulled his coat over his head, not feeling prepared to welcome the day yet. He heard his name, spoken in a sweet, musical voice, and remembered where he was.

He opened one eye and looked out the window. Abigail smiled and motioned for him to open the door.

Davey did so as she stepped back, and was greeted with a warm blanket and a silver thermos.

"I thought you'd like some coffee. Are you hungry?"

He covered a yawn and accepted the warmth. "I could eat," he said with a chuckle.

She smiled. "Give me about fifteen minutes."

Davey blinked, becoming more aware of his surroundings. The truck had lost its initial heat hours before, so the blanket was a welcome comfort. *How did she know to find me here?*

He wasn't far from the house, but he couldn't see it from where he had parked. *I need a better parking place if I'm going to protect her. Maybe I should just call the cops.* He reached for his nonexistent phone. *Really, Papa?* He frowned. *She shouldn't spend one more day with that man.*

Davey glanced in the direction of the house, wondering if Nathan had left for work yet. *He must have, for her to risk coming here.*

He turned to Abigail. "I've been known to cook a little..."

She shook her head. "I appreciate the offer, but there's no need." She closed the door before he could object, and returned to the house.

Davey started the truck and followed her slowly. He rolled down the window. "Want a ride?"

She laughed. "It's not far."

"It *is* cold, though."

Abigail looked at the snow surrounding her. "It's beautiful. Just look at those trees."

He did, and she took off in a run. "Race you to the house!"

He watched her disappear around the corner and laughed. He turned slowly behind her—obviously letting her win.

"You're not even trying!" she shouted as she ran faster.

Nathan's car squealed as he left the driveway. Davey slowed until he'd rounded the corner.

Abigail climbed into the passenger side of his truck when he pulled into her driveway. "There are scrambled eggs inside."

"Does your husband...?"

"He's going to work. He won't bother you."

"I know—but I mean—are you going to get in trouble when he gets back?"

She shrugged. "It's hard to know with him. Sometimes he's cheerful; sometimes he's not. Will you come inside?" Abigail looked around his truck.

He noted with amusement her attempt to withhold judgment. "Nice place, right?"

She smiled slightly. "So...you live here?"

Davey chuckled. "Sometimes."

"It's...nice."

He laughed, and she joined in. "My mom thinks I need a new one."

"Truck or house?" she grinned.

"Truck," he said, smiling. "My actual house isn't bad." *It's not up to Mical's standards...but it's not bad.*

"But the new trucks have no character," Abigail said, her eyes still smiling. "I mean, look at this." She picked up the cover of the glove compartment, which had long since refused to stay closed. "I challenge you to find any new truck with a feature like that."

Davey nodded sincerely. "I'm with you," he agreed.

Abigail smiled, shifting and tucking her legs underneath her. "Uncle Sammy told you to take care of me, didn't he?"

"Asked," Davey admitted.

"Yes, but he knows no one has the heart to say no to him, so it's basically the same thing."

Davey chuckled. "I suppose that's true."

"You don't have to stay, you know."

"I know."

"You can go back, and tell him everything's okay. I'm healthy...and we'll have a little one soon."

"I know."

She watched him for a moment. "You're still planning to stay here, though."

"Yep."

She smiled. "I suppose we'll need to get some food in you, then. Come on."

He followed her inside, and she handed him a plate of scrambled eggs mixed with bits of bacon. "I ate with Nathan," she said. "But there are more eggs in the pan if you would like them. There's more coffee, too."

He thanked her and began to eat.

She sat across from him and watched him as he took a bite. "You're just as stubborn as he is, you know."

Davey chuckled. "I suspect you are, too." He drank the last of the coffee in the thermos.

Abigail jumped up to give him a steaming mug as a replacement. "Now, whatever gave you that idea?" She laughed, not loudly, but unashamed. As she set the mug by him, he noticed the swollen area around her eye was getting worse.

I need to get her away from that man.

Her expression softened as she sensed his changed mood and guessed where he was looking. "It doesn't hurt," she said, as if that made it okay—and as if he would believe that.

"How often does this happen?" Davey asked.

Her silence was enough to tell him it was a regular occurrence.

Davey set his fork down. "We're getting out of here."

"Davey, no."

"I will not stand around and let him hurt you again. Think about your child." He stood, gathering a handful of supplies in a plastic bag.

Abigail put a hand on his arm. "Don't, Davey."

"I'm not letting you stay here. Not with that man."

"That man is my *husband.* I'm not leaving." She pulled the kitchen towels and spoons from the bag. "By the way, you have the worst idea of packing I've ever seen."

"You owe him nothing, Abigail." Davey added more to the bag.

"I never said I did." She took the bag from him before he could make more of a mess.

Davey shook his head. "You seem so smart when it's not about him, Abigail..." He frowned.

"You don't know what he's like," she began.

"Oh, I'm sure he's fantastic when he's not beating you and putting your child in danger." Davey didn't even attempt to keep the sarcasm out of his voice.

Abigail shook her head. "That's not what I mean at all. I know it's wrong, what he does. I've seen real love—I know that's not what this is."

He crossed his arms. "Then why…?"

"I want to leave; I do. I tried once already." She rolled up her sleeve, revealing a bumpy series of deep scars starting at the inside of her wrist and moving to her elbow. "I was hospitalized for three days."

Davey looked at her eyes, which were fixed on her scars.

"I can't risk him hurting my little one," she said.

He nodded, finally understanding her position. "What if I could get you out safely? He would never find you."

It was the first time he'd noticed pain in Abigail's smile. "If you can find a way to make that happen, I would go. I would welcome it."

Davey smiled. "I'll find a way."

"I wouldn't put that on you…" she began apologetically.

He put a hand on her arm, covering the worst of her scars. "You have your little one to think about now."

She nodded. "Exactly."

"It will be okay," Davey said. "I promise."

Abigail turned away and looked at the empty bag. "Want to help with cleanup?" Her smile returned as she looked at him.

Davey chuckled.

"Seriously… What were you preparing for here?" She lifted the dish soap and ceramic plate he'd included and shook her head, amused.

"I don't know…I just took what I saw."

"Clearly. Remind me to teach you what the essentials actually are sometime."

As she put the last part back where it belonged, she directed him back to his unfinished eggs. "Want them heated?" she offered.

"I'm sure they're fine; thanks."

She brought his coat and a blanket to rest near the heater and poured him a fresh cup of coffee. She placed a carton of cream and a bowl of sugar on the table before pouring herself a cup. "Can I get you anything else?"

Davey smiled. "You remind me of my mom...she loves playing hostess—as long as someone else does the cooking."

She smiled.

"You've already given me everything I could want. You're great at this. Do you have people here often?" He glanced around at the kitchen.

"No, not often—not at all, really. I'd love to, though."

He nodded, distracted by what he saw around him. The Trenkets owned many of the appliances he'd seen in Mr. Benson's kitchen: a large electric mixer, an espresso machine, and a food processor, among others. They were all on his 'someday' list. "Where does Nathan work?"

"He owns a jewelry store in the town next to this one."

He's an entrepreneur. So he's successful—or very in debt.

The interior of the house didn't match the outdated and worn outside. It reminded him more of a mansion than a farmhouse, with a baby grand in one corner and quality wood carvings on every visible surface. He motioned to an especially intricate piece decorating the edge of the counter. "Did you do that?"

Abigail looked where he was pointing and laughed.

She has the most beautiful laugh.

She shook her head, still smiling. "I wouldn't even know where to begin with that kind of thing."

Davey smiled. "Neither would I. My dad used to bring me to the wood pile in the park—you know, where people would make bonfires. When I was upset, he'd give me a knife and let me do whatever I needed to with the logs."

"Really?"

He nodded. "Now that I think about it, giving a knife to an angry teenager is a pretty bad idea...but it helped." He chuckled. "So, that's my experience with carving. Beautiful things don't tend to come out of angry hacking, though."

Abigail laughed again—there were no weak giggles with her.

"The reason I asked is because the last house I was in that had that kind of woodwork had been done by the ladies of the house. I'm afraid I insulted them with my surprise when they told me...so I figured I'd be safe this time."

"I don't blame you for being surprised—I wouldn't have expected it, either."

"So you're not a secret craftsman. What else should I know about you?"

Abigail's eyes smiled and she stood. She walked swiftly past him and out of the room.

Did she want me to follow? Davey took a swallow of his coffee to give himself a moment to decide.

She returned before his moment had ended. "This is what I do in my spare time...and I have plenty of that." She placed a handful of necklaces across the table and surrounded them with rings, bracelets, and pairs of earrings.

"Does Nathan sell these in his store?" Davey asked; he wasn't sure the proper way to admire jewelry.

Abigail shook her head. "When we were first married, he gave me beads and rolls of wire to make them, and said if they were 'good enough' he would sell them." She lifted one of the necklaces, a simple one with a mix of silver beads and small green jewels. "This one almost was."

Davey looked at it. It seemed perfectly fine to his untrained eyes.

"But there's always something. Something that's not just the way he imagines it." She shrugged and genuinely seemed not to care. "Eventually I stopped showing him, and he stopped asking."

"Yet you still make the jewelry?"

She nodded. "I realized I enjoyed it, even if nothing happened to the results. Now I make them and take them apart to reuse the beads. It might be a waste of time...but I like it."

Davey smiled. "That doesn't seem like a waste at all."

Chapter 10

Mical woke to pains near her stomach—more than the nausea she had become used to. It almost felt like cramps, but was different, in a way she didn't feel up to figuring out.

She closed her eyes, hoping that in a moment it would go away on its own.

Ten minutes later she was still grasping her stomach.

Her phone rang: Peyton.

Work.

She slid it open to answer.

He didn't wait for her greeting. "Listen, Mickey, I don't mind staying here during your shifts until you get more comfortable working alone, but I'm *not* going to work in your place unless I'm the one being paid for it."

Mical groaned a little.

"You're fifteen minutes late. What do you have to say for yourself?"

He was trying to be funny, but she could see no humor in it. She also couldn't form words. Tears came to her eyes.

There was a slight hesitation, then, "Are you okay, Mical?"

She swallowed and whispered, "I don't know."

"I'm on my way." He didn't hang up.

She heard surprised complaints as he apparently ushered customers out with, "You can come back later," and, "just take it; it's on me." He spoke into the phone again. "I need your address, Mical— or a description of your house. Anything."

Struggling, she managed to give him basic directions. Her house was close enough to walk to; finding it shouldn't be difficult. She clenched her jaw as she walked to the door and unlocked it, then slid to the ground and sat beside it. There was no chance of returning to her room.

A few minutes later, Peyton came in. He found her, curled into a ball. With a little effort, he leaned beside her and picked her up. Mical was in too much pain to even try to protest as he carried her to his car.

"You're just going to have to suffer through my junk-mobile for a few minutes," Peyton said in apology as he turned the key. It sputtered, hesitated, and groaned as it started.

They reached the hospital, and Peyton carried her in. He explained the situation to the receptionist and scowled when she directed him to the waiting room and asked him to sit with Mical. "If she gives birth while we're in there, I'm holding you responsible," he said with only a touch of humor.

It's too early for me to give birth, Mical tried to say it out loud, but a lump in her throat prevented words from forming. *I can't have the baby this soon!*

By the time the nurse led Mical to a room, the pain had lessened and she felt able to leave the hospital, but she stayed to learn why the pain had happened.

The nurse told Peyton to wait in the lobby until they were done.

She asked Mical some basic questions about her health, learned how long she had been pregnant, and asked whether she'd had an ultrasound yet. After another half hour, the doctor came in, asked many of the same questions, and ordered a full ultrasound.

The pain came in waves, but the tests took so long that it was almost completely gone when they had finished.

The nurse named some medical reasons for the pain; Mical didn't try to understand or remember them. The doctor looked at the results of the ultrasound, but her face gave away nothing. She told Mical to take it easy for a while and said everything would be fine.

Mical left, feeling only slightly comforted.

Peyton was waiting for her in the lobby, but said nothing as they walked to the car. After a few minutes of silence on the ride home, he asked, "What did they say?"

I don't feel like talking about this, Peyton. She shrugged. "They said I'm fine."

"And the baby?"

"Also fine."

Peyton smiled. "The pain seems to have lessened. How are you feeling now?"

Mical sighed in frustration. "It doesn't hurt anymore." *But I'm also not in the mood for a chat,* she wanted to add. *This was too much like losing my baby, and I just want some time to myself right now. And I wish you were Anna.* She would understand the need for silence.

Peyton had another question for her: "So, your choice. Where are we headed?"

"What do you mean?"

"Well, are you feeling up to working a shift now, or would you rather head back home? I can cover at the gas station if you need me to."

She hesitated. She needed the money, but wanted the rest. *The money matters more right now.* "Work. I'm fine."

He nodded.

Take it easy. Like that's ever going to happen. Not with Davey gone, anyway.

Peyton turned into the gas station and parked the car. He unlocked the doors and turned on all the lights.

"You left it empty?"

"What choice did I have?" he smiled. "But don't worry. If the manager gets upset, I'll take the heat for it."

She shook her head. "You will not. You'll tell them exactly what happened—or send them to me and I will. If they don't understand, I'll deal with it."

He shrugged. "They're pretty easygoing in general. I wouldn't worry."

"I'm not worried." She slipped behind the counter, pinned her badge to her shirt, and waited for customers to start arriving.

Peyton stepped beside her. "Sorry—" he started, pushing some of her hair behind her ear.

Mical stepped away from him. "What are you doing?"

"It was kind of sticking up."

"Then you *tell* me."

"Right. Sorry. Your hair is kind of sticking up. Well, not so much now."

She rolled her eyes. "Go get your book, twerp. Or you can leave, if you want."

"You're not going to freak about being here on your own?"

She glared at him. "I have never 'freaked'. I merely pointed out that I hadn't been trained."

"And after one day, you think you're trained sufficiently?" He pursed his lips suspiciously.

"If it means getting you out of here..."

Peyton laughed. "Aw, and here I thought we were getting along."

He risked his job for you; be nice, Mical. "Sorry," she mumbled.

Peyton got comfortable on his chair in the back. "Used to it," he said with a wink. "Besides, it's probably the pregnancy talking now."

Mical laughed. "You can tell yourself that if it makes you feel better."

"I just might." He grinned. He turned his attention to his book, but only for a moment. "Hey, were you there on Tuesday? I missed that class."

She nodded. "It was mostly just discussion... I took notes. You can copy them if you want."

"Awesome." He hunched over his book as a young woman and two small children entered the store.

Mical tried not to be a stalker and watch them while still making it known she was available if they needed her help. It was a difficult balance to achieve.

They picked what they needed and paid for it as well as some gas, then left.

"Were you working that day?" she asked, turning her attention back to Peyton.

He shrugged.

"Hey."

Peyton looked up from his book. "Yes?"

"I thought you were going to quit the act."

He smirked. "You don't think I'm just naturally nonchalant?"

"Hardly." She grabbed a cloth and wiped down the counter.

"Maybe I just like being mysterious."

"If by 'mysterious' you mean 'a turd', I'll believe it."

"A turd? I'm hurt. You can't come up with a more creative insult than that for me? I'm your favorite person to pick on!"

She giggled a little. "I thought it was creative. Poking fun without being overly mean, you know."

"Yeah? Hmm."

She smiled and tucked her hair behind her ear. She could get used to this side of Peyton. She could even start to like it, if it was his real personality.

I wonder what his real personality actually is. He seemed sincere now. *He didn't seem sincere before. Just dull.*

A middle-aged, balding man walked in and interrupted her thoughts. He searched the gum display but frowned when his first choice wasn't there. He named his preferred brand of cigarettes and waited as Mical retrieved them from behind the counter.

"Thought you were gonna quit that, Vic," Peyton said, startling the man.

He smiled somewhat guiltily. "Well, I thought you were going to get some bubblemint gum here, so I'd say we're even."

"Hey, I tried. It's up to management what flavors we have here. It's up to *you* to take care of yourself."

Vic laughed. "I suppose you have a point there. Nonetheless, I'd still like the cigarettes."

"Don't say I didn't warn you when doc gives you the bad news," Peyton said, shrugging a little.

Mical looked at him, then at Vic, not sure what she was supposed to do.

"Just the cigs, dear. Thanks."

She scanned them into the machine and gave the man his total.

Vic paid with a credit card. "And don't you be judging me, Peyton. I know enough of your own bad habits to write a book."

He laughed. "Point taken, Vic. See you when you run out." He winked as the customer turned and left the store.

Mical turned to him. "So...you know each other."

"He's a regular here. You get to know them after a while."

"How long have you worked here?"

He shrugged. "Too long."

"That isn't an answer."

He chuckled. "It's been about two years. I keep considering moving to a new job, but I don't. Not many places around here are willing to hire someone before he gets a degree, you know. Well, I mean, you must...you're working here too."

She made a face. "Do you hate it?"

He shook his head. "It's a good job to have. Good managers, decent customers. That's about all a college drop-out can ask for."

"You're not a drop-out yet." She hesitated. "Are you?"

"Not officially."

She nodded a little. Davey had helped her keep school a priority, and with him gone she was realizing just how much of a sacrifice that had become for him. *He could easily tell me it wasn't possible, but he knew I had my heart set on it.* Maybe that's why he'd continued to work for her father. *He didn't want to risk not being able to support my dream.*

She bit her lip at the thought.

"You okay there? Need another fun trip to the emergency room?"

Mical smiled slightly. "Not yet."

"Good, because I'm not sure my car would make it that far."

She giggled. "I doubt it'll make it out of the driveway, even."

"Hey—only I can knock my car."

She crossed her arms. "Really?"

He chuckled. "Nah, I know it's junk."

Mical smiled. "Well, I don't even have a junk car, so I'm not making fun of it. Much."

"David has one, doesn't he? Where is he, by the way?"

"Davey? Um...he's on a trip."

It was Peyton's turn to raise an eyebrow. "You know I can see right through you, right? And I'm a curious sort, and I'm also a little bit bored right now, so..."

She sighed. "It's complicated, and it's a long story."

"Marital troubles?"

"No."

He closed his book and set it on the ground. "I can keep guessing until I hit on it, or you can just tell me. Eventually I *will* get it out of you."

"You really are bored today." She glanced at the clock. *Just one more hour.*

"His great aunt is sick?"

She laughed. "No. You can make a million guesses, but I bet you'll never get the actual reason for his absence."

"He's pretending to be a homeless man for a while?"

"Um...no. What?"

He shrugged. "I've considered it. Just to give me more empathy when I pass them."

"Okay. That's...nice...I guess."

He shrugged. "He's having an early mid-life crisis and needed a trip around the U.S. to get through it?"

She shook her head, smiling. "Not even close."

"He just couldn't stand his in-laws anymore and had to get away?"

"That's...not terribly far off, actually." She turned her attention to the register, opening the drawer to count the cash and compare it to the expected total.

"Okay. I'm close." Peyton tapped his finger on his mouth. "Do you have any other hints for me?"

She shrugged a little.

"Do you just not want to talk about it?"

"I'd kind of rather not, yeah." She frowned, picked up the twenties, and started counting them again.

"Okay, I'll drop it. For now."

"Thank you." She moved to the pile of tens.

"You know, we usually don't count that until we're ready to close the store. Then we're able to get our ending total."

She restarted counting the tens.

"I'm distracting you and messing up your counting, aren't I?"

"Very much so." She sighed, picking up the money again and beginning once more.

"Well, let's see what other topics I can bring up to distract you more..." He paused, then said, "52. 29. Seven."

"Don't you have a book to read, or a phone to play games on, or something?"

Peyton laughed. "I do...but where's the fun in that?"

She put the money back in the drawer. "When do our paychecks come?"

"At the end of the week. Friday morning."

She calculated how many calls she would need to make before that day came. It was Tuesday; she could last four more days if she needed to.

Chapter 11

It had been three weeks, and Davey had settled into a sort of routine. He had a sore back from sleeping in the truck, and was losing more sleep than usual, but nothing beyond that made him want to stop. His mission, as he had begun to think of it, wasn't complete yet.

Before Nathan came home, Davey would move his truck to a nearby street. He'd walk back to the house, and wait in the shed—close enough to listen, but still hidden.

At any sign of trouble, he was ready to jump up and protect his dear friend. Perhaps Nathan knew this, and that's why there hadn't yet been a reason to reveal his presence. As long as Abigail and her baby were safe, the reason why didn't matter. He would continue until he found a way to get her out for good.

The shed was cold, even with the heater Abigail had placed inside when she learned what he was doing. When the lights in the house turned off, Davey returned to his truck.

In the morning, he would wait until after seven, when he knew Nathan would be at work again, before driving to the house once more.

Abigail made him breakfast and coffee.

"What was your favorite Christmas, Davey?" she asked when she learned it was the holiday he loved most.

He considered. "One Christmas, we headed to New York to visit my dad's parents. Grandma Laura had knitted Robbie and me each a scarf, and Mom insisted on making us wear them all day long to show our appreciation."

Abigail smiled, getting up for a moment to refill their mugs.

"Well, if we had been celebrating Christmas outside, that wouldn't have been a problem—but in the comfy, fire-warmed house, it was."

She laughed. "I can imagine. Why is that your favorite memory?"

"Oh, you asked for favorite. I thought you'd said *least* favorite." He chuckled. "I actually loved that Christmas, just because it was one of the few times we got to see Dad's parents. We lived somewhat close to Mom's—about two hours—but were 1,000 miles from my other grandparents. What was your—"

The door swung open and slammed against the wall, putting a dent in the sheetrock. Nathan's eyes narrowed at Davey and Abigail, who had been sitting on the couch, talking.

He stomped forward, tracking mud and snow through the kitchen. Davey stood and stepped in front of Abigail.

"Out of my way!" Nathan easily shoved Davey to the side and pulled Abigail to her feet.

"Leave her alone, Nathan," Davey said, forcing his voice to remain calm. "She's done nothing wrong."

Nathan scowled at Davey. "I will deal with *you* later," he spat.

Davey stepped in front of Abigail once again. "No, you will deal with me *now*." He shook his head. "Actually, I will deal with *you*. No one deserves to be treated the way you have treated your beautiful wife." He turned to Abigail. "Call the police and wait outside."

"What?"

"Just do it," Davey said, turning his attention back to Nathan.

Abigail pulled out her phone as she left the room.

Nathan balled his fists and, using a mixture of colorful language and formulaic threats, ordered Davey to leave.

Davey remained calm, but closed his own fists in preparation for the attack.

The man had a different method of fighting in mind, however. He reached over the end table for the knife Abigail had used to cut cheese that afternoon.

Davey stepped back. *What now, Papa?*

Nathan lunged, and Davey dodged. Davey aimed for the knife, and Nathan sidestepped his grasp. Nathan outmaneuvered Davey and sliced the side of his shirt.

He bit back a groan as he felt the effects of the knife on his side. He covered the area with a hand. It was wet but not deep. *Keep fighting. Don't stop. Don't let him win.*

He stood—a new determination in his movements.

Nathan tightened his grasp on the knife and dove toward Davey. "You think I don't know the lies you've been feeding my girl?"

Davey stepped to the side, letting Nathan's attack fall on the sofa cushion. "Abigail hasn't been yours since you first stopped treating her with kindness and love," he said, his voice even as Nathan adjusted after his failed swing.

"So you thought you'd jump in where you saw an opening." Nathan charged again, narrowly missing Davey's temple.

Abigail returned from outside. "Nathan—stop!" She ran to his side and reached for his knife-wielding arm before he could strike Davey again.

Nathan's anger changed directions. "And *you*," he faced his wife, eyes narrowing. "You, who promised until death—you, who claimed to love—to love *God*—" He advanced on her, nerves bulging. "If separation is what you are after, death is the only way I will grant it!"

Abigail stepped backward and tripped over one of the coffee table's legs, landing on her back with a panicked scream.

Davey had taken Nathan's momentary distraction as an opportunity to move from prey to hunter. He reached from behind Nathan and wrapped his hand around the knife, effectively aiming it at Nathan's neck.

Abigail stared at the two, scrambling into a seated position against the side of the couch as she watched.

Davey could feel pressure against his hand as the knife reached Nathan, and he let it rest there. He hoped the fear of death would be enough to stop him from attempting another attack.

Papa... Police?

Nathan was too wrapped in anger to relent. He struggled violently against Davey.

Not wanting to truly hurt the man, Davey released and threw the knife against an open wall. It bounced off and landed on the floor, several feet away from the duel.

Nathan cursed and spun to face Davey. He struck, hitting Davey in the side. Davey punched Nathan in the gut in retaliation.

Nathan came at him again, using only his fists this time. Davey lunged at Nathan, and caught him in a headlock.

"Let's end this," he growled, catching him in a chokehold he'd learned from his days as a thief. It wouldn't kill him; it didn't even affect his airflow. All it would do is knock him out for a moment, which would give them time to plan their next step.

Abigail scrambled for the knife, but didn't move once she had it.

The police arrived as Nathan sunk to the ground. Davey, drenched with sweat and trembling from the aftermath of the fight, joined him, still conscious, on the ground.

The officers assessed the situation: Nathan motionless on the ground; Davey beside him; and Abigail, quaking and sobbing, holding a knife.

One officer knelt beside Abigail, said some calming words in a voice too quiet for Davey to hear, and, with a gloved hand, put the knife into an evidence bag. Another stepped beside Davey and Nathan, took a quick glance at Davey, and checked Nathan's pulse.

"He's fine," Davey said, breathing heavily. "He's just unconscious."

"He's dead."

"What?" Davey strained to get a better look at Nathan. "That's not—that's not possible."

"Murder, Jeff?"

He grunted an affirmative. "I'd say a pretty clear case of it." He clapped a set of cuffs on Davey as he spoke.

The officer beside Abigail, who a moment before had been kind and compassionate, put handcuffs on her as well, and led the two of them out as Jeff prepared Nathan's body to be moved.

Every step hurt. Every breath was filled with more pain than air. His side had already stopped bleeding—it was barely more than a scratch—but something wasn't right.

"Stop being kind to the criminals, Mark," another officer scoffed as they made room for Nathan's body in the other car.

Mark shrugged. "They're still people." He frowned at the obvious pain on Davey's face, but didn't care enough to find another option. He put a hand on Davey's head to push him the rest of the way into the back of the squad car.

Abigail had tears in her eyes. "Davey—"

The cuffs made it impossible to hug her, but he moved closer anyway. "It's okay," he said; his voice was quieter than normal. "I'm sorry this happened."

Mark got in the passenger side as Jeff started the car.

Abigail turned to the officers. "Davey's been hurt. Let me do something—please."

They looked at each other as if considering it but shook their heads a moment later. "No can do, lady," Jeff said.

"He will receive proper medical treatment when we get to Ellsworth."

"That might be too late!"

Davey shook his head. "I'm fine," he said, though the pain right above his stomach disagreed with the assessment.

Jeff looked at the other officer as he moved the car out of Park and began to drive. "This looks like a crime of passion to me," he said, and Davey noticed the beginnings of a satisfied smile reach the corners of his mouth.

Mark nodded in agreement. "She's more upset about her *friend*'s flesh wound than about her husband's death."

Davey wished he had more strength to defend Abigail, but even just breathing was becoming difficult. She didn't deserve the false accusations implied in their words. He turned to see how she was reacting, and took in a sharp breath as he felt another stabbing pain inside.

Abigail's eyes filled with tears and she pulled against her restraints, trying in vain to come to his aid.

"Which one of you did it?" Jeff asked, apparently oblivious of their struggles. "You will make this whole process much easier if you confess right now."

"Easier for who?" Abigail spat the words.

"All of us, I would imagine."

Davey closed his eyes and focused on the voices.

"We're not going to confess something we didn't do," Abigail said.

"Oh, I believe *you* didn't. You're just the witness. But you can still be helpful," Mark said. "Just tell us what your boyfriend did, and maybe the sentence won't be quite as harsh."

Abigail let out a breath of frustration.

"Of course, we could always bring out the evidence against *you*," Jeff said, in not nearly as kind a tone. "We did find you with the murder weapon in your hands."

"M-murder weapon? This isn't a murder!"

Jeff continued: "I bet you don't want to be in prison when Baby Trenket arrives. Do you know what happens to prison babies? They get placed in foster homes. We wouldn't want a generation raised by murderers, would we?"

Shut up. Just shut up. Davey couldn't force his mouth to speak the words—not from fear or respect, but from a physical inability: an intense weakness he had never before felt.

"Did you even *look* at the body?" Abigail's voice was growing louder and higher with her level of distress. "The knife didn't *touch* him!"

"Seems like she knows what did, Mark."

"Of course she knows. We just have to find the soft spot that will coerce her into telling us."

"That shouldn't be too difficult. Withholding medical treatment from her boyfriend would probably do the trick."

"What?" her voice was a high-pitched squeak.

"What did I tell you?" Jeff laughed heartily.

"You—you can't," Abigail continued in a more reasonable but still urgent tone. "That would be an abuse of your...of your power."

"We are here for justice," Jeff said, undaunted. "And that is what we will achieve, one way or another."

"I will not be coerced into a false testimony," Abigail said resolutely.

"Then you have decided your boyfriend's fate."

"Jeff, that sounded so great. I'm writing that one down to use later."

They laughed.

"I've been waiting for the right moment to use that line." He turned too quickly and the car jerked in protest.

Davey's teeth gritted to keep his scream down. *Stay strong for her.*

"Feels good to have some action around here," Mark said.

They chuckled together.

Abigail stomped her foot. "You can't do this!"

"Honey, when we're in this uniform, we do what we want." Davey could hear the smug grin in Jeff's voice.

"You aren't even being logical!" Abigail's voice was becoming shrill again. "We're the ones who called you! Check my phone if you don't believe me. Why would we call if it meant turning ourselves in?"

There was silence for a moment.

"She has a point," Mark said, beginning to relent.

"But the fact remains that we have a body, a murder weapon, and two people with plenty of motive. All we need is the how."

"You'll find that in the autopsy," Abigail said, calmed by Mark's willingness to admit fault.

"You seem certain about that. What do you believe we will find?" Jeff asked.

"I don't know. That it wasn't murder. That there was no reason to take us in like this."

"In our position, would you have done any different?" Mark asked.

Davey was growing sleepy, but tried to focus on the conversation.

"Maybe," Abigail said.

The car went over a bump, jostling the passengers. Davey thought he heard a small crack—maybe he'd felt one. The voices grew softer, and eventually faded into silence.

Chapter 12

The holidays were over, and school had begun once again. Chrissy, Anna, and Mira had each invited Mical to spend Christmas with their families. Instead, she'd spent it at the gas station, then alone in her house. She took down her sparse decorations before the day had even ended. She was glad the season had passed; now she could focus on the truly important things: school, work, and the fact that her baby's arrival was nearing. She glanced at the calendar. *Six more months...give or take.*

Mical rubbed her eyes as she tried to focus on the words in front of her. *Just one more chapter and I can sleep.*

She was trying to settle into a schedule: school in the morning; work in the afternoon and into the evening; and studying at night—but it was becoming more difficult with each hour of sleep she lost.

What if this is unhealthy for my baby? She shouldn't even be *having* a baby. Until a couple of weeks before, she hadn't even dared to hope for one.

Someone had been wrong, and as much as she wanted to believe it was her doctors throughout the years, the odds weren't in her favor.

She felt her stomach, hoping for a little movement to ease her fears, but nothing came.

Come on, little one...you have to make it.

Mical almost didn't answer her phone. The number wasn't in her contacts, and there was no reason for anyone else to call. Besides, it was after eleven. She wanted sleep, but needed to study, and neither involved picking up her cell.

Still, she answered after the third ring, right before the voicemail caught it.

"Is this the Blake residence?"

She nodded. "Yes...who is this?" Mical released a silent yawn as she waited for the response.

She heard only breathing on the other end for a moment.

Prank caller. She yawned again and moved the phone away from her ear to hit 'End'.

"Miss..." the voice was slow, almost forced.

She held the phone up again. "Yes?"

"I'm with the Ellsworth Police Department. I understand your husband was David Blake?"

She hesitated. "Yes...?"

"I have some bad news."

Mical listened in silence as the officer explained.

"There was nothing we could do," he said, his third or fourth cliché since the conversation began. "I'm sorry."

She swallowed, not wanting to comprehend his words—not wanting to accept them as truth.

"Ma'am?"

"Yes?"

"Where can we send his things?"

She hesitated. "Can I come get them? Can I see him?"

The officer's voice held surprise. "Of course. I mean—his body isn't viewable—it's pretty gruesome—but you can get his things."

"I'll be there tomorrow," she said. It meant skipping class and owing Peyton yet again as he covered her shift at the gas station.

She looked at her call history—her last hope that this was a scam. The second search result confirmed it as the number of the Ellsworth Police Department.

She slammed the laptop closed and covered her face with her hands.

When it was nearing four the next morning and Mical was certain she had no tears left, she texted Peyton a request to open the store for her. She didn't wait for a return text as she pulled a sweatshirt over her pajamas and started searching for the keys to the truck.

After about five minutes, she could feel the tears returning as she remembered that Davey had the truck—it was already in Ellsworth, or wherever he had been last. She hesitated for only a moment before dialing Chrissy's number.

Chrissy picked up after the second ring, her voice slow, quiet, and slightly nasal—a confirmation that the call had awakened her.

"I'll have you know, Mically, you are the *only* person whose call I would take this ridiculously early in the morning." Her tone was forcibly amused, with more than a touch of irritation.

It was enough to bring on a new wave of tears.

"So I hope you have a good reason. Like, your nonexistent dog is sick, or you forgot where you put your favorite pencil."

Mical shoved her emotions down with a difficult swallow. "It's...Davey..." she managed.

"I'm on my way. Keep talking, or not—whatever you need. I'll put you on speakerphone while I drive."

Mical could hear the tinkling of Chrissy's overly full keychain and a moment later the roar of her car's engine.

She knew Chrissy deserved an explanation for the early morning interruption, but she couldn't force her mouth to make the words.

"You don't have to talk, Mically," Chrissy said, reading the silence on her side of the phone call. "I'm sure it will all be clear soon enough, and—" she let out an exaggerated yawn, "—and I'm sure you're in no mood to talk about it right now anyway. Do you want me to talk, though? Because I can. Or I can be quiet. Whichever you need."

Mical blinked away new tears, and bit her lip.

"I'm going to take that as an affirmative that you want the distraction of my loquaciousness—isn't that a fantastic word? I just learned it. Um, anyway, if I'm reading your silence wrong, go ahead and start whining or something." She paused, presumably to give Mical a chance to start making noises, but continued when she was greeted with more silence.

"So I got a scholarship notification in the mail. Apparently someone from the clothing store I work at put my name in for one—isn't that sweet of them? It's a very generous offer—not a full scholarship, but a good amount. But I won't be able to use it. I'm working more now, and really enjoying it—I mean, it takes some pretty awesome coworkers to even think of submitting my name to a scholarship contest. And it's really helping at home. The extra hours, I mean. We might be able to keep our house if they keep scheduling me as often as they have been lately!"

Chrissy paused to take a breath before resuming her speedy chatter. "On Friday it was Robin's birthday—you know, one of my younger sisters—oh, of course you know! Man, I can't think straight before ten in the morning. I have to be up by five thirty for work sometimes, so you'd think I would be used to early mornings by now, but I really think that isn't something you can learn, you know? You're either a morning person or you're an 'I hate the world until lunchtime arrives' person, and I'm totally the second. Oh—and I'm here."

Mical stepped outside and joined Chrissy in the car before she had unbuckled.

"I need," she took a deep breath. "I need to go to the Ellsworth Police Department. In Wisconsin." Mical rubbed her temples. "Can I borrow your car?"

"What's the address?" Chrissy reached for Mical's phone and opened the navigation app.

"I...I don't know." Her throat tightened again.

"Oh, that's okay. We'll find it." Chrissy tapped something into the phone and a moment later a calm, electronic voice gave the first instruction. "Sorry for just grabbing your phone like that. I would use mine, but it's so old I'm lucky to even get texts on it."

Mical dug into her pocket and pulled out a couple small bills and some loose change. "This should get you to work or home, or wherever you need to be today. I'll bring your car back in a few hours."

Chrissy shook her head. "No offense, but I don't really want you to drive my car in your emotional state. It's probably not great to drive it in my sleepy state, either, but you pick your battles sometimes. So buckle up and get comfortable. We have an hour long drive ahead of us, according to your ever-so-helpful GPS app."

Mical didn't try to argue. "Thank you."

Chrissy smiled and left the driveway. "I love car rides, you know. When I was younger and gas cost less, my family used road trips as our main form of entertainment. For a while we'd go just about every weekend. Not far, of course, but an hour to five hours away, and it was always an adventure. We'd play games like 'I Spy' and sing songs together.

"Oh, we weren't always happy about it. There were some trips I *really* didn't want to go on, sometimes when the thought of spending hours in a cramped car with no air conditioning made me want to puke, and some days when I actually did."

She smiled a little sheepishly. "I suppose that was too much information. Sorry. All in all, though, I loved those trips, and I miss them now. I have so many happy memories from them."

Mical turned and looked out the window, watching but not noticing the trees and buildings and other cars zooming by.

"You still have the option of growling if I'm talking too much—just so you know." Chrissy let out a small giggle, which was quickly stifled by a yawn. "You never really did road trips with your family, did you? I guess your family wasn't really the kind to go on them. Mira would always choose staying home, and your father had his business to worry about."

Chrissy turned the radio volume down. "I don't imagine he would have been willing to leave that in anyone else's hands, even for just a few days. I would hate to be tied down to something like that, wouldn't you?" She glanced at Mical, then laughed. "Well, maybe you wouldn't mind it, since your dream is to open a business of your own! But you aren't like your father. You don't share his lack of trust—at least not to the extreme that he has it. I'm sure you'll be able to find someone to run your business when you and Davey go on trips."

She adjusted the heat. "Speaking of going on trips with your darling—the two of you never really had a honeymoon, did you? Life just kind of started happening as soon as you said 'I do,' right? We'll have to fix that sometime. Well, *you* will. It wouldn't be very romantic if I was tagging along."

Mical was glad she was facing away from her friend as tears found their way down her cheeks for what seemed like the hundredth time in only a few hours.

Chrissy continued, unaware of Mical's emotions, or unable to guess the reason for them.

"How long has he been away now? It's been a few months, hasn't it? I bet you miss him. Is he at the police station? You must be beyond excited to see him again. What do you plan to—"

"Can we talk about something else?" Mical asked it more forcefully than she had intended.

Chrissy paused for only a moment. "Of course. I'm sorry. Do you know if Jonathan likes to travel? He always struck me as the type that would enjoy it, but it's something I was never able to confirm."

Mical shrugged.

"I mean, it doesn't matter whether he does or not. It's not like we would ever get to travel together. I was just curious. So I guess you've been pretty busy lately, with work and school—and your tummy is starting to show! Maybe only because I know—you're not too far along, are you? Does Davey—" she stopped herself and changed the direction of the conversation. "Anything else? Oh, did you know my sister Cathy is dating now? It sure makes a person feel old when their younger siblings start getting into romantic entanglements! Well, it does for me, anyway. But he is a really nice guy—no, not nice. He's a *good* guy. I don't care for the term 'nice' anymore. Any person can be 'nice', you know. It's the special ones who deserve other adjectives. Don't you agree?"

After a while, Chrissy gave up trying to include Mical in a conversation, and turned the radio up to sing along.

Mical propped the side of her forehead against the cool glass and closed her eyes. Chrissy had never been comfortable with silence, and at that moment it was a trait Mical was grateful for. She'd had hours of quiet the night before, and knew it only made the pain worse...though even Chrissy's nearly incessant chatter wouldn't make it better.

The hour passed, and Chrissy pulled into the police station parking lot. "I don't see Davey's truck here..." Something seemed to click in her mind. She put a hand on Mical's arm. "Is Davey in jail? I know Jonathan thought your father was trying..."

Mical shook her head, and Chrissy must have noticed the tears filling her eyes. Her tone softened even more. "Mical...what's going on?"

She still couldn't form words, but Chrissy seemed to understand that it wasn't the time to ask.

"Alright, well, let's go in and get this sorted out." She waited outside the car while Mical gathered her emotions.

Mical took a deep breath. *Just go in and go out. Make sure this is...real. Maybe it's a mistake.*

She looked down at her hands, then pushed the door open.

An officer looked up from the paperwork on his desk when they entered. "Can I help you?"

Mical glanced around the station before responding. It was a small, plain, brick building. There were three metal desks inside, with papers falling off of them. The walls were covered in outdated, painted metal, filing cabinets. *I wonder which file is his.*

She forced the words out. "I was told I could pick up Davey—David Blake's things here. I'm...I was...I am...his wife."

The officer's eyebrows drew together and he sucked in a short breath. "Yes—of course—we spoke last night. I'm so sorry." He stood, removing his hat and revealing a bald spot near the back of his head. "I'll be back with his things in just a moment."

Chrissy put a hand over her mouth, everything sinking in at once. "Oh, Mical..." Already, tears began to form.

Chapter 13

"What do you suppose happened?" Mark examined the results of the autopsy with a critical eye. "I wonder if these things are ever wrong."

"They're not."

He swiveled his chair to face Jeff. "You don't know that."

Jeff shrugged. "Does it really matter?" He picked up an especially large pile of papers on his desk and started organizing them.

"What's with you?" Mark stood and leaned over Jeff's desk, sliding the results under his nose. "Look at this."

"Don't put that here unless you want it moved to a file." Jeff turned in his chair, his back to the other officer.

Mark picked up the paper again, shaking his head. "This doesn't belong in a file. More like in the shredder."

Jeff glanced over his shoulder, his eyebrows lifted incredulously. "I thought you didn't want to get in deeper with this."

Mark frowned and started to pace. "We're already in," he said. "Now we just need a way to stay in."

Jeff shrugged and focused on the filing again.

"At least we released the girl. Fingerprint proof or not, prison is no place for a pregnant woman. Besides, the knife isn't what killed him."

He continued when Jeff didn't respond: "Too bad about her friend, though."

"We can only do so much," he said, barely audible.

"Yes, but we could have done more."

Jeff stood and began separating the documents in the filing cabinets that lined the room.

"I also don't like that we used threats to try to force a confession. That isn't procedure."

"We've never had a case like this before. There *is* no procedure." With a click, he closed a drawer and slid another open.

"Still. I don't feel right about it. Any of it."

"We were only doing our job and keeping our part of the deal."

"But...that man's wife..."

"She'll be fine," Jeff snapped. He put a paper in the wrong file and swore under his breath.

Mark frowned.

Jeff looked up after a moment. "She called him Davey, didn't she?"

Mark shrugged.

"I was told his name was David."

"One is just a nickname for the other," Mark said, turning to his own work.

"I'm not stupid, Mark. The point is, his father-in-law called him David. Why wouldn't he refer to his son-in-law by his nickname? Don't families usually use more friendly names for each other?" Jeff set the papers aside and looked at Mark.

"Well...I would hardly call this family a close one. Besides, maybe Davey is his wife's pet name for him. My wife calls me—well, she has a special name for me when no one else is around." Mark chuckled noncommittally.

"Davey is more a childhood nickname—one that's used regularly—than a name used only by his significant other. That would be something like Pookiebrain. And didn't Abigail Trenket call him Davey, too?"

Mark shrugged. "We did suspect them of being more intimate than just friends." He returned to his desk and glanced at his own overflowing pile of papers, seeming to consider tackling them. He took a drink of Mountain Dew instead.

Jeff shook his head. "Nothing matched up for that to be the case. I was merely using that as a tool to try to put her on the witness stand. Protecting one's reputation can be a very large motivator."

"Apparently it wasn't large enough."

Jeff went back to filing. "She valued maintaining the honor of a man she'd met only a few weeks before more than guarding her reputation against false rumors."

Mark looked up, his eyebrows lifting and scrunching together at the same time. "How do you know they met recently? They seemed like old friends."

"His father-in-law told me."

"Oh." Mark emptied his can and pulled a new one from his bottom desk drawer. "What did his wife ask when she was leaving? She spoke so quietly I couldn't hear from my desk."

"She wanted David's keys," Jeff said, his frown remaining. "He didn't have them with him when we took him in."

"What did you tell her?" Mark opened the can and gulped his pop.

"I said I didn't know where they were and couldn't help her." Jeff shrugged.

"So you lied."

He turned to Mark, and his eyes narrowed. "No, I didn't."

"You know exactly where the keys are. At least, you know a highly likely location."

"Yes, and that would lead her to Abigail, which would lead her to—"

"—the truth. You lied." Mark smirked before swallowing another mouthful.

Jeff shrugged again. "I prefer to look at is as doing what was necessary."

Mark watched him for a moment. "You weren't so hardened before we started all this, Jeff."

"Neither were you."

"I don't like what we're doing. We could get into trouble."

"We knew that when we first agreed to this, Mark. We knew it was wrong and knew the risks, but the compensation made it worth it. To me, it still does." He looked critically at Mark. "You aren't backing out now, are you?"

Mark hesitated. "I have my boys to worry about, Jeff. They can't have a corrupt police officer for their role model!"

"I hate to be the one to tell you this, but they already do." Jeff left the file drawer open as he sat at his desk.

Mark scowled. "They at least can't know about it."

"So who's going to tell them? I won't. Will you?"

Mark shook his head.

"Simon, you, and I are the only people who know about the deal. If any one of us squeals, we'll be incriminating ourselves as much as anyone else. That's how Simon wanted it," Jeff said. "And," he added, "it's brilliant."

"I suppose..."

"So just quit worrying." Jeff's tone remained calm, but the way he moved pens and paperclips around his desk revealed his true feelings.

"I wasn't prepared to make two widows, Jeff. I didn't even want to make the one."

"Nathan deserved what he was given," Jeff spat. "It's nearly done, anyway. All that's left is to testify."

He slammed his nearly empty can on the metal desk. "And say what?"

"What we saw and what our conclusions are based on that."

"And we'll just ignore this?" Mark shook the autopsy results at Jeff, and his eyebrows lowered, shading his eyes in displeasure.

"What difference does it make? Either way it was murder. He was strangled, or he was a perfectly healthy, twenty-six-year-old man who had a heart attack. Both point to murder, and death by strangulation gives us the murderer."

"David Blake. The man he knew for only a few weeks."

Jeff shrugged.

"I would rather not commit perjury under oath—especially as an officer."

"Abigail had every possible motive and opportunity to sneak poison into Nathan's meals. Do you really want to pull her into this again?" Jeff's voice was growing louder.

Mark considered. "Sure, if you think she's guilty."

Jeff gave a small shrug. "Between a convicted man and a pregnant woman with no record, my bet will be on the criminal every time. But sometimes I'm wrong."

Mark began to pace. "If she's innocent, the court will see that. If she's not, she deserves jail."

Jeff slammed his fist on the desk and shouted swear words at the other officer.

Mark stood in one place and crossed his arms in front of him, defensive. "What is your problem?"

"She didn't deserve *any* of this! Look. This is her file." He tossed a manila file folder onto Mark's desk. "This wasn't her first call to us."

"Okay..." Mark scratched his forehead.

"Every month or two she'd call for help. Whoever was running the phones here really messed up. They added her name to a file, reported it as domestic abuse, and forgot about it." Jeff cursed again.

Mark glanced through the file.

"At one point, she even ran. Do you know the courage it takes for someone in a position like that to do that?" Jeff shook his head. "We don't get many cases like that here, but I've seen it. They feel trapped."

Mark let out an impatient breath as he sat down and dropped the file onto his desk. "Your point?"

"We got a call from Nathan: a missing persons report on Abigail. That's in there, too," he motioned to the file. "But that's the one we *didn't* ignore."

Jeff slammed his fist against the top of the desk again. "We found her, and brought her back to the one person she wasn't safe with. We're the problem, Mark—or we at least added to it!"

Mark nodded. "But we didn't know..."

"That's the whole point, though, isn't it?" Jeff's lips drew together in disgust. "We're called protectors, and we failed to protect. She deserved better, and she still does. Guilty or not, I will not incriminate her. Nathan Trenket got the justice he should have, and I am perfectly content to leave it at that."

The other officer shook his head. "It's murder. Someone has to pay for it." Mark frowned. "I don't feel right sending an innocent man to jail for something a battered wife did."

"He isn't innocent, whether he committed *this* crime or not. He's guilty of many other crimes. I would much rather see him behind bars than her."

"Sure, anyone with a heart would, but that doesn't make it right."

Jeff scowled. "If Abigail poisoned her husband, she had a perfectly good reason to. She isn't going to hurt anyone else. Who knows what else the criminal has in mind."

"But Jeff, if she did it, it was self-defense. The jury would see that, and the judge would let her off without a charge."

"This isn't a traffic ticket, Mark. They don't pass out warnings for murder, no matter what the motive was." Jeff shook his head. "And I won't risk seeing a perfectly excusable crime being punished to the full extent of the law because you were too much of a coward to follow through on a promise."

"Why does this Samson guy care, anyway?"

"*Simon* cares because he doesn't like seeing his daughter with that man."

Mark shrugged. "It still feels wrong."

"Which will let you sleep easier at night, Mark: putting away a possibly innocent pregnant woman or putting away a decidedly guilty criminal?"

"It isn't fair to word it like that, Jeff. And you're forgetting about the *criminal*'s wife. She, at least, is innocent. Why did you lie to her?"

Jeff stomped his foot, somehow managing maintain adult maturity while he did. "I didn't lie! Did you listen to the conversation at all? I never once said something that wasn't true."

"You just highly implied an untruth. Why add that complication to the rest of this? What happens when she learns the real story?"

"I did her a favor, Mark."

Mark laughed loudly. "Oh, I would love to hear your rationale behind *this*," he said. "How, exactly, did you do Mrs. Blake a favor?"

"I spared her from having to learn just what kind of man she married. Instead of knowing him as a murderer and a thief, she will have him in her memory exactly as he was the last time they spoke. I've let her keep her good memories."

"What about when he is convicted?"

"There will never be a reason for her to find out."

Mark frowned. "You think it's not going to come out? Newspapers love this kind of thing—and you really think her father isn't going to tell her? He seems more like the type who would flaunt it."

Jeff shrugged. "My part in this is done, and nothing you say is going to make me regret the decisions I have been forced to make."

"I'm not a murderer, Jeff."

"Neither am I." He leaned back in his chair.

"Why aren't you more concerned about this? Why do you have no guilt?"

"I shouldn't need to explain this to you again, Mark." Jeff let out a frustrated breath. "Think about it this way: Would you rather your wife believe you were dead or believe you were in prison?"

"I would want her to know the truth."

"What if you died while being brought to prison? Still want her to know the truth then?"

Mark shrugged.

"Would you really want her to be told the circumstances of your death? I think you'd rather she remember you as the hero you had been until that moment. I think most men would."

"Apparently, David wasn't much of a hero even before this."

"Not in her eyes. She was blinded by love, so the little she knew about his past didn't seem so bad to her."

"I still don't like it," Mark said.

"You've made that very clear."

Chapter 14

Textbooks lay unopened on the floor around the bed. Mical's phone blinked from at least three unread and unheard messages. Her stomach complained of hunger; it didn't have the same resistance to needs as the rest of her body.

Mical rolled over, ignoring all of it, and pulled the covers past her eyes to block the afternoon light.

There was another knock at the door. The doorbell rang a moment later—the third time. Whoever it was had been there for at least fifteen minutes. Mical had initially hoped they would leave under the impression that no one was home.

She groaned loudly, picked her robe off the floor, and started running fingers through her hair.

They caught on one of the many knotted clumps, so she scratched her ear instead of fighting it.

She knew without looking in a mirror that her face was blotchy and her eyes betrayed a lack of sleep. She half coughed, half sobbed into her elbow before opening the door.

Peyton blinked and said nothing for a moment.

Mical sighed. "I know they fired me. That's what happens when you don't come in for three days. Did the school kick me out, too?"

Peyton shook his head. "I've been covering for you at the gas station—and you know how seldom the managers show up. Your job is safe. And our teachers never really took attendance anyway. Are you sick?"

"Sure, let's call it that."

"Morning sickness?" Peyton guessed; his nose scrunched as he said it.

"No."

"Those awful cramps again?"

Mical tapped her big toe, not willing to play Twenty Questions with him. "Did you need something, Peyton?"

He hesitated. "No, I guess not."

Mical closed the door without a word and went back to the closest thing she had to a sanctuary: her bed. She sought comfort in a sleep that was reluctant to arrive and fitful at best.

Hours later, she jumped as a gentle touch woke her from a dream about Davey.

"Sorry," Chrissy said, her voice soft. "The door wasn't locked, and it was easier to just come in without knocking...and I knew you wouldn't answer if I tried calling."

Mical blinked and looked at her, willing the sleep out of her eyes.

Chrissy's eyebrows drew together in a mixture of compassion and shared pain, without even a hint of pity. Mical wasn't the only one who lost someone special when Davey died.

Mical forced herself to sit up as Chrissy joined her on the bed. They wrapped each other in an understanding hug, and Chrissy held on until Mical's next wave of tears subsided.

She sat back and looked at her friend. "I brought food. I know you don't want it right now, and I don't really, either, but I bet your baby does."

Mical nodded and moved her hand to her growing stomach—her baby.

Chrissy retrieved her bag from where it had landed on the ground and took out a couple peanut butter sandwiches. "I'm not a good cook like you are," she said apologetically, "and we didn't even have jelly, so I used honey instead. But I figured it would be better than nothing."

Mical took one in silent gratitude. She pulled the crust off and chewed slowly.

"Have you picked out a name yet?"

She shook her head.

"I guess you won't know if it's a boy or girl until later. Do you have a guess?"

Mical shrugged a little and swallowed. "I'm hoping it'll be a boy...but I think it's a girl."

"Why?"

"Just a feeling," she said. "I don't think any of the silly tests people suggest are accurate, so I haven't tried any. I just think it will be."

Chrissy nodded. "Why are you hoping for a boy?"

Mical lowered her eyes. "Because that's the only way...I mean...he'd...he'd look like Davey, at least a little."

Chrissy nodded again.

"I didn't deserve him, Chrissy."

Naturally, she opened her mouth to object, but Mical stopped her with a slight shake of her head.

"I lied. All of it was a lie. Because I knew he wouldn't accept me with the truth—but—it wasn't his fault."

Chrissy chewed on her lower lip. "What are you talking about, Mically?"

She picked at the strings of the blanket to avoid Chrissy's questioning eyes. "He wouldn't have married me if he'd known I wasn't a Christian. And he deserved to know I wasn't. What I did to him was wrong."

Chrissy said nothing as Mical continued.

"I was selfish. I wanted him, and didn't think about at what cost. And once we were married, and he learned about it, he no longer had the freedom to back out. I mean, I don't know what your religion says, but he wasn't willing to consider a divorce."

Mical didn't look to see Chrissy's response.

"He was nothing but loving to me, Chrissy, no matter what. He should have been given the same in return."

Chrissy remained unnervingly quiet for a moment. Mical finally risked a glance at her friend, expecting judgment.

Instead, Chrissy put a hand on her arm. "You love him so much—you still do—and he never questioned that. I don't believe he regretted marrying you, whether or not he would have if he'd known all the facts. And I know he wouldn't want you to hold onto this guilt. He loved you, Mical. Not the *idea* of you."

Mical brushed a stray tear on her sleeve. "I miss him, Chrissy. I missed him before, but this is so much worse. It should be easier, shouldn't it? He'd been gone for so long." She took a shaky breath before continuing. "But it's not. It's impossible to do anything without being reminded of him—and then—" she swallowed, "—reminded that he's gone."

Chrissy pulled her into another hug, sensing the fresh tears before they had fully formed. "We're always going to miss him. It's always going to hurt," she swallowed down her own tears. "And even knowing he's with Papa isn't much of a comfort because it doesn't feel...*fair*—for Papa to get him for eternity when we were only given a few years."

Mical nodded and wiped a sniffle into the Kleenex Chrissy offered.

"And I know no one ever needs platitudes or empty promises that 'things will get better,' so I won't give you those. But I want you to know I'm here—as often as you need me."

A few days later, after missing more than a week of work and classes, Mical forced herself to clean up and join the others on the city bus once again. She pored over her textbooks as an excuse to avoid conversation with the other passengers. *Not that there was ever a real danger of it with this group.*

Anna ran to her as soon as she entered the school and captured her in a hug. She held her tightly for a moment. "Oh, I've missed you! I know it was only a week or two, but it felt like more." She released Mical and stepped back to look at her. "How are you doing? I called a couple times and left messages, but Peyton said you didn't seem to want visitors. Maybe you just didn't want *him*. I should have stopped by—I'm sorry I didn't."

Mical shook her head. "He was right this time. But...I'm...well, I'm a little better now."

"Is it the baby?" Anna asked; her voice was barely audible with her concern.

Mical shook her head. "The baby is healthy." *At least, I think it is.* She'd been too busy or too nervous—perhaps a mix of both—to visit the doctor in the last couple months.

"Are you going to make me play a guessing game here?"

"It's Davey," Mical said.

Anna nodded slightly, but the way she pursed her lips and drew her eyebrows together showed that she wanted more information. "You have some time before your class starts, don't you?"

Mical checked the time on her phone. "About fifteen minutes."

"We'll make that work," Anna said, leading her to their study spot. From a habit of playing hostess, she offered Mical a mint, which she refused.

Mical sat on the couch and clasped her hands in front of her, elbows on her knees.

"So...what happened?" Anna sat next to her, back against the arm of the couch, legs crossed in front of her.

Mical stared at her hands and considered the easiest way to tell her. *Just say it.* "He was in a fight...broke a rib...and he didn't make it." She swallowed as her throat started to tighten.

Anna didn't even attempt words. She pulled Mical into a hug.

"I tried so hard not to believe it," Mical said. "I even went to Wisconsin—to the police who found him. I don't know...I guess I hoped I'd get there and it would be nothing but a misunderstanding. Like, they'd give me someone else's things, or they'd ask me to identify the body and it would be someone else. But it wasn't a misunderstanding. It was him."

Anna rubbed Mical's arm, letting her speak.

"They said he was protecting a woman from her abusive husband when it happened." Mical couldn't help but smile at that. "It's so like him. He never could stand and watch as innocent people suffered. He always had to stick his nose in...never worried about the consequences."

"He was a good man," Anna agreed, "and he died a hero."

"He lived a hero, too," Mical said.

"I'm so sorry, Mical."

She checked her phone again. "I need to get to class." She stood up. "Thanks, Anna."

That afternoon, Anna stopped by with a basket of fresh cookies and three large containers of still-steaming meals. "I figure this should last about a week and give at least a little variety," she said as she filled Mical's fridge. "There's milk and eggs and cheese in the car if you want to grab those. Just the staples, but it might save you from a grocery trip this week."

As Mical retrieved the rest of her friend's gift, Anna placed a variety of coffees and teas on the counter and set a kettle of water on the stove.

The two sat on the couch, savoring the aroma of their liquid warmth.

Mical wasn't ready to revisit the subject of her husband's death, and Anna seemed to realize that.

"Did Peyton tell you what he's been up to this past week? Or, rather, what has happened to him?"

Mical shook her head. "I guess I didn't really give him the chance when he was here...and I haven't been checking my messages lately. Did he get kicked out of school?"

"No; actually the opposite happened. Well, it's kind of an opposite."

"What do you mean?"

"He just inherited some money from a cousin— enough to buy a house, pay for school, take care of his family...I mean, he's not rich or anything, but he can quit working until he graduates. Then he'll be able to get the kind of job he really wants."

"That's great." Mical was only slightly sincere. "So now he really is just slacking off."

Anna's forehead scrunched together. "What are you talking about?"

She shrugged. "He wasn't in class today."

"Oh...I suppose he wouldn't have had a chance to tell you that part, either."

Mical swallowed a too-warm mouthful of coffee. "What part?"

"He's been working your shifts at the gas station so management doesn't hire someone to replace you."

She blinked. "He's still covering for me?"

"He said he will until you no longer need it," Anna said.

"But...why would he do that?"

"I have some theories." She set her mug on the coffee table and tucked her legs underneath her. "But the main reason is that he knows you need the job. He doesn't know about Davey yet, but he knows you've been hurting. He can't soothe it like girls can try to, but he can make sure you don't have the added stress of needing a new job. He's a good guy, Mical."

She nodded thoughtfully. "I guess I've been learning that."

"If you're feeling up to it, he's working this afternoon. I know he'd love to see you."

"Do you want to come?" Mical asked.

Anna shook her head. "I'd better not. I actually have a paper due in the morning, and it's only half done right now. I should probably finish it at some point." She smiled. "But that doesn't mean I have to leave now—unless you're ready for me to go. You rank higher than a silly paper. Peyton...nothing against him, but he ranks lower today."

Mical giggled softly.

Anna smiled again as she picked up her mug and sipped her tea. "Ooh...perfect temp. Try yours now and see if you agree."

They talked for another hour, until Mical decided she should thank Peyton for holding her job—and let Anna return to writing.

The bell over the door made a feeble attempt at a jingle as she entered the gas station.

Peyton looked up from his textbook and smiled. "You're looking better today."

"Hey," Mical said, "Anna told me you've been working my shifts still...and I know that meant you had to put school off...and I know you no longer need the money from this place..."

Peyton shrugged. "I don't mind."

"Well...I only work here because I need to. And I need it now more than ever. And I don't think I would work shifts if I could afford not to... Anyway, thanks."

"You're welcome, Mical." He smiled. "So, do you want your job back, or do you still need some time?"

"I can start again," she said as she pulled some crumpled, loose papers from her bag and handed them to him.

"What's this?" he asked.

"My notes from class today. Sorry I don't have them for the rest of the week."

"Thanks Micke—Mical."

She smiled. "You can call me Mickey if you want to."

Chapter 15

Mark and Jeff sat in the break room, shuffling a deck of cards for another round of gin rummy.

"I suppose someone should check on the prisoner," Mark said, more a comment than a commitment.

"It's your turn," Jeff said.

Mark frowned.

"He's asleep, don't worry. He's always asleep. He's still recuperating from the broken rib."

"I'm not afraid of that," Mark said, but the tremble in his voice said he was.

Jeff rolled his eyes. "You owe me one." He unlocked the office door and glanced at the prisoner.

Davey sat directly in front of the door and watched as the man reached for his gun. "I'm not dangerous," he said. "Besides, like you said, I'm still recovering from my wounds."

Jeff scowled. "How long have you been awake?"

"Off and on, since you first brought me in here," Davey admitted. "I've heard a lot of conversations I'm sure you never intended me to."

"Oh really?" Jeff's voice was monotone with a forced mix of disbelief and sarcasm. "Like what?"

Davey considered, weighing the pieces that would give him leverage. He'd been among these kinds of men before. The uniforms were the only thing that separated them from his former gang. Their actions and words were nearly identical.

Jeff closed the door and pulled a chair up across from Davey. "What have you heard?" he demanded.

"I know who you're working with," he said. "I know what you told my wife."

Jeff laughed. "That'll get you far."

"You made a deal with Simon Benson, which ended in the murder of Nathan Trenket." He leaned back in his chair, and tilted his head at the officer. "You also lied to my wife. I'm content with what I can do with that information."

Jeff frowned for a moment. He shook his head and a nervous smirk replaced it. "Well, no one will believe you. You're nothing but a criminal."

"What proof do you have of that?"

Jeff blinked. "Proof?"

"You keep throwing the accusation out. I assume you've researched it and have proof to present to the judge at the initial hearing on Thursday." Davey's lips twitched, fighting his own smirk. "You *have* done that, haven't you?"

"It's easily found."

"You have a computer somewhere in this building, don't you?"

"Of course," Jeff said, annoyed by the obvious question.

"Bring it in here, and show me even one piece that tells you I'm a criminal. I would love to see it. In fact," he chuckled, "we can have a race. I'll bet you a prison sentence that I can present proof of your misdeeds before you can find it of mine."

The officer scowled. "I don't take orders from people like you."

"Right," Davey chuckled. "You just take them from people like Simon Benson. Get the computer or I'll expose you and your partner for the crooked cops you are."

"You don't know a thing about either of us," Jeff said. "You have no right to judge."

He shrugged. "Perhaps you're right. You're simply illegally holding me here on fabricated charges. But, you're right. I have nothing to base judgments on."

Jeff crossed his arms.

"There is one thing I'd like to know, though. Who really killed Nathan? I know it wasn't Abigail, so don't even—just don't." He narrowed his eyes at Jeff.

"I wouldn't," Jeff said. "I'm the reason she was released."

Davey laughed loudly. "No. The reason for *that* was because no jury would convict her. Maybe you did it." His lips drew into a thin line as he watched the officer.

Jeff shifted in discomfort, but didn't show guilt.

"Maybe Simon did," Davey continued, still closely watching for a reaction, "though I don't see him as the type who would get his hands dirty."

Still, Jeff revealed no new information.

It doesn't really matter at this point, anyway. He tried a different tactic. "Abigail has every right to sue this place for failing to protect her. Based on how the paint is cracking and the carpet is filled with coffee stains, I'm guessing the budget wouldn't have room for that...which means there could be

151

cutbacks. I would make sure they started with you."

Jeff crossed his arms. "I'll get the computer. But not because you told me to; because it'll get you to shut up."

Davey chuckled. "You do that."

Jeff left the room and locked the door, and Davey could hear the two officers arguing about Jeff's decision.

After the conversation grew quiet, Jeff entered with a laptop. He set it on the empty desk and started searching through police files.

"I can make this very simple for you. I lived in Backus until I was ten, then moved to the twin cities. I haven't been anywhere but there since then, and I came here three weeks ago. But you knew that last part already."

Jeff ignored him as he continued to search the entire database.

"Do you think I care if you believe me?" Davey chuckled. "I really don't."

Jeff continued searching. His scowl etched deeper when more and more results came up empty.

"I told you there would be no proof," Davey said with a satisfied smile. "Don't trust everything Simon Benson tells you. The reward money he promised...have you seen a penny of it yet?"

"That's none of your business," Jeff said.

"So there *was* a reward promised. That's interesting."

Jeff slammed the laptop shut. "I'll find the proof," he said. "I'm not worried about that."

"Here's the thing, Jeff. I'm not willing to go down for a crime I didn't commit." Davey rested his elbows on his knees as he leaned forward on the folding chair. "There are autopsy results that prove I couldn't have done it. I'm sure the judge will be interested in those."

Jeff frowned. "What do you want, David?"

"I want my freedom. I want Abigail's safety. I want what you claim to want: justice."

"The only real justice would be to put Simon Benson in prison."

At least we agree on something. Davey leaned back again. "That's not likely to happen."

Jeff set the laptop on the floor beside him and scratched his day-old stubble. "Why not?"

"He's too careful. You'll find even less on him than you have on me. What's the next option?"

"Look—" Jeff pulled out his cell and scrolled through messages. "I have all the proof I need, right here. Recorded phone conversations, check stubs, handwritten instructions..."

Davey's heart rate skipped and sped at the possibility. "What do you want in return?"

"Complete anonymity as the source. I don't want to be implicated in any of this."

Davey ran his hand through his too-long hair as he considered. He stood and walked to the small window of the office. *I could finally protect Mical.* Jonathan would be given power in the company. *I could return home without fear.* He and Mical could go back to their lives.

Davey blinked. He wasn't sure he *wanted* to go back to that. The fighting, the lies, the emotions...and what would happen to Abigail when he left Diamond Bluff? What was happening to her now? She was strong, but she had never lived independently.

A thought returned: *If I had met Abigail before I met Mical...things would be different.* Another thought took its place. *Things could still be different.* Mical had mentioned divorce... *And why not? The entire foundation of our marriage was based on a lie.*

"Think about it," Jeff said.

Oh, I am. Davey forced himself to focus on the officer. "What about Mark?"

He shrugged. "If you can find a way to keep his name untarnished, do it."

Mark opened the door and looked in. "Hey, um, there are like five people here who want information about David. What should I tell them?"

Jeff scowled. "Tell them what you told his wife!" He called Mark some unpleasant names before slamming the door in his face.

Davey stood and walked to the door to listen.

Jeff watched him. "You really can hear from in here, can't you?"

He nodded. "Every word."

"Who are they?"

A smile curled Davey's lips as the familiar voices met his ears. "My family."

"Oh." Jeff glanced at Davey. "Think about it," he said again. He stepped around him and walked out to send the unwanted guests away.

He picked out his parent's voices and Robbie's, and smiled. *I love you guys.*

"I'm sorry, but the body wasn't viewable," Jeff said when one of them asked to see it.

Isn't it a little late to be asking for that, anyway?

"Okay, then where did you bury him?" Joe asked.

"We have flowers—" Ella said, her voice strained.

Oh, Mom...it's okay.

"Well, he hasn't been buried yet..."

Davey's smile grew as his family's questions broke down the lies Jeff and Mark had been spreading.

A new voice spoke: "He's been dead for more than a week and you haven't buried him yet?"

Jonathan. *I've missed you, bud.*

"We felt it should be up to his widow where he was placed," Mark said, his voice shaking.

"Well, where is his body then?" Robbie asked.

"It isn't here," Jeff said: not really an answer.

Davey tried to open the door. It was locked, but the noise of the failed attempt gave him an idea. He shook the handle and pounded on the door.

"What is that?" Joe asked.

"Who's in there?"

"Oh—that's just one of our prisoners. Don't worry about it."

Davey couldn't make out the rest of the conversation above the noise he was making. He stopped and stepped back as the door opened.

"Davey?"

He grinned. "I knew you'd show up eventually."

"Davey!" Ella's tears turned to joy and she pushed the others aside in her excitement at seeing her son.

Joe, Robbie, and Jonathan didn't bother to hide their smiles as they waited for their turn to hug him.

After the initial greetings, Jonathan turned to Jeff and Mark. "I'm not even sure where to start with you. Just know that you will regret this."

Ella noticed the bandages across Davey's stomach—the best the doctors could do for his broken rib. "Has that been looked at?"

He nodded. "They brought me to the hospital first."

"At least you did *one* thing right," Robbie said, his fists balling with the growing sense of injustice. "You have a jail literally one mile from here. Why are you keeping him in an office?"

"It's because they don't have real charges against him," Jonathan said, scowling.

Joe frowned. "He's coming with us." He put his arm around Davey and started leading the group out.

"No—wait—you can't—" Mark faltered.

"This is illegal," Jeff said, blocking their path.

"You want to talk illegal?" Robbie's voice squeaked.

"Talk to my sister, you jerks," Jonathan said. "You know: the one whose heart you broke with your lies." He pushed Jeff out of the way as the others continued to the cars.

"We will be pursuing this," Robbie said, "so don't worry—you'll see your prisoner again. It'll just be from the other side of the bars."

Davey spoke up as they pulled out of the driveway. "Wait, Dad. There's someone I want you to meet before we go."

About fifteen minutes later, they pulled into the Trenket's driveway.

Abigail answered the door with a smile and wrapped Davey in a hug. She quickly pulled away when he gasped at the touch. "I'm so sorry, Davey—I'm so sorry for everything."

Davey he hugged her again, more gently. "You were not at fault for any of this."

"Except, maybe, terrible taste when it came to picking a husband, right?" She laughed.

Davey chuckled. "Abigail, I want you to meet my family. Mom, Dad, this is Abigail. Robbie and Jonathan are in the other car."

"I've heard so much...it's so good to meet you." She distributed hugs to both his parents and waved to the guys in the car.

Ella motioned to the "For Sale" sign in the yard. "You're moving?"

She nodded. "I can't afford this place on my own...and I wouldn't want to stay here after...everything."

"Where will you go?" Joe asked.

She shrugged. "I haven't thought that far ahead yet. I suppose I'll just see where God decides to take me."

Joe and Ella exchanged a look; they both nodded.

"Come stay with us until He leads you else-where," Ella said. It wasn't a command, but it was firm.

"Are you serious? You don't even know me."

"Davey does, and that's enough," Joe said.

Ella nodded in agreement. "We have an entire basement just begging for someone to use it. It's not ideal, I'm sure, but it's a good-sized space for you and your baby."

Abigail hugged them again. "You don't know what this means to me. Thank you. Thank you *so* much."

"Can we help you pack?"

Abigail nodded. "I don't need much."

Joe motioned for Robbie and Jonathan to join them as they brought out the essentials from Abigail's house.

Less than an hour later, they were back in the cars and on the way home.

"I need to stop somewhere else before we go back," Davey said. "There's someone I need to settle things with."

Joe frowned. "What do you plan to tell Mr. Benson, Davey?"

He shrugged. "I figured that would come when I get there."

"Can I watch?"

Davey chuckled. "Sure, Dad."

Chapter 16

Mical replayed the offer in her head, wondering if she'd made the right choice. It had been more like a business deal than a proposal. She could sell her house and use the money to pay off her debts.

She would have her own space—the entire upstairs. It wasn't huge, but there was a private door leading to it, and enough room for her and Angel. She could even have her own kitchen if she wanted one, he'd said.

But it would still be a marriage.

She'd said yes, reluctantly. It seemed like the only option. At her current salary, she couldn't afford an apartment, and she'd lose the house even if she didn't sell it. At least this way she could use the money for debts and college, and could start saving for her own place again.

She wished she knew someone else she could stay with. Anna, Chrissy, Mira...none of them had the space, especially once Angel arrived.

Her feelings for Davey would still be there when the wedding day arrived in two weeks. She doubted she could love anyone as much as she loved him.

Peyton assured her that he knew that, but wasn't willing to offer the space without the marriage—people would talk, and he wanted to keep her reputation intact.

Like they won't talk if I remarry less than a month after my husband dies?

Still, she saw his point.

Besides, the baby needs a father figure. Peyton was a decent guy after all; she wouldn't mind him as a role model for her little one. The thought brought her hand to her stomach, and there was a tiny bump of acknowledgement. Mical smiled.

I love you too, Angel.

She would go through with it—all of it—for her baby.

The doorbell rang. Mical opened the door and smiled as Chrissy stepped inside.

"Angel moved."

"Really?"

"Just now," Mical said, a proud smile inching across her lips.

Chrissy put a hand on Mical to see if it would happen again. "Angel must know I'm not mommy," she said a moment later, then gave Mical a belated hug. "How are you doing?"

Mical shrugged. "I mean...it doesn't go away. I have a feeling it's not going to."

Chrissy nodded as she moved to the kitchen and put a pot of water on the stove for hot chocolate. "Do you want coffee?"

"I have some...thanks." Mical retrieved her mug from the table.

"Oh...you have another visitor," Chrissy said, motioning to the window. "Do you know whose car that is?"

Mical stepped closer to look, expecting Peyton's rust bucket. Instead, she saw a silver BMW she didn't recognize—the kind of car her father would drive; but that dark brown hair was too long to be his.

She squinted to see the face of the driver.

"I'll take that as a 'no, I don't know who that is,'" Chrissy giggled.

Mical shrugged. "It's an 'I can't recognize people from the back of their head' more than anything."

"Really?" Chrissy turned around. "You wouldn't know that was me?"

Mical laughed and shrugged. She looked back at the window in time to see Anna pull a bag from the passenger's seat.

"I wonder what she wants..." Chrissy said. "Do you know her?"

"Of course," Mical said. For a moment, she was surprised that Chrissy didn't. "That's Anna, from the U."

"Oh—I finally get to meet a friend from school! Well, besides Peyton." Chrissy's nose bunched together when she said his name. She watched Anna walk up the steps. "She's in classes with you?"

"Yah. Some of them, anyway." Mical headed to the door before Anna had a chance to knock.

"What do you think she wants?" Chrissy asked, shadowing her.

"Same thing you do," Mical shrugged.

"So...hot chocolate."

Mical blinked and looked at Chrissy.

She laughed.

Anna smiled and hugged Mical. "How are you doing? Oh—I know that's a dumb question. Here," she held up a plastic bag. "I brought some snacks."

Chrissy leaned her chin on Mical's head. "I don't know you yet, but Mical said your name is Anna. I always thought Anna was such a lovely name! I mean...it's the last part of my full name—so I *should* like it. It's nice to meet you." She pulled her new friend into a hug.

Anna smiled and returned the embrace. "Well, thank you. What's your name?"

Chrissy laughed. "Oh, silly me. I suppose that would be good to know, too. I'm Christiana—but most people call me Chrissy. Is Anna short for anything?"

"Nope...I'm not cool enough to have a nice nickname like the two of you."

Mical scrunched her nose. Micaela wasn't a name she appreciated. The only person who had ever used it was her father.

Anna stepped inside and placed the grocery bag on the counter. "Ooh," she said when she saw the teapot starting to steam. "Can it be tea time?"

Chrissy grinned and matched her excitement. "It can be if you want it to be! I prefer hot chocolate...and Mically has her, um, coffee."

The two exchanged an almost frown at the last word.

"There is nothing wrong with coffee," Mical said, her tone a little higher in defensiveness.

"Sure—if your taste buds are broken," Chrissy giggled.

"Exactly!" Anna agreed.

Mical rolled her eyes and turned away. *How am I supposed to make them understand this?*

"I can handle it with lots and lots of sugar," Chrissy continued. "Not too much, because then it just tastes like...sugar. But enough to disguise the grossness. It's a delicate balance."

Anna smiled in response, but her attention had moved to Mical. "Is something new happening, dear?"

She hesitated, which brought Chrissy's curious eyes to her as well. "What is it, Mically?"

Just say it. She did.

They stared at her. Chrissy opened her mouth, but no words came out.

Anna seemed suddenly interested in her cup of tea. Her voice was unnaturally quiet. "Why?"

"I'm going to lose the house. This way I have somewhere to go—and it gives me control over when it happens."

"Two weeks?" Chrissy said, regaining her speech. "How am I supposed to plan a wedding in two weeks?"

Anna looked at her. "It's not that kind of wedding, Chrissy. At least," she returned her eyes to her cup, but there was a question in her words. "At least, I don't think it is."

"It's not," Mical assured her. "It's—well, it's that I have Angel to take care of—and I can't do everything alone."

"But we're here, Mically."

"You have as much to worry about as I do, Chrissy. And you," she turned to Anna, "are moving after this semester."

Chrissy frowned. "What about Mira?"

"Don't you think I've thought this through?" Mical asked, tears coming to her eyes. "Do you really believe I would do this if there was another way?"

"I'm sorry," Chrissy said quickly. "I didn't mean...it's just..."

"It's marriage. I know."

Anna stirred her tea with the diffuser, still refusing to lift her eyes. Her voice remained quiet, almost inaudible, as she spoke. "People married for convenience in the past. Sometimes it turned into more. Sometimes it didn't. Either way...there's no reason for us to be judgmental about it now."

Chrissy nodded. "I really didn't mean to be, Mically—I'm sorry."

Mical nodded. "So...Peyton's coming over soon. So I just wanted you to know that before he gets here."

Anna set her cup on the table, and her spoon rattled against the edge. "I...I have to go. I'm sorry." She stood and briskly walked outside, leaving no opportunity for the usual goodbye process.

Mical blinked, surprised by her exit. "I guess she doesn't approve," she commented.

Chrissy mouth moved to the left, and she seemed to be looking at nothing. "I think," she said, "Anna has...other reasons. It's not because of you. At least, that's not the only thing."

She was too exhausted to try to interpret Chrissy's uncharacteristically vague language.

"When did he ask you?" She moved to the counter and pulled out a container filled with cookies. "Oh, I like this girl. There's both chocolate chip and peanut butter with Kisses." She started to arrange them on a plate.

"Last night," Mical said.

"Did he get on one knee?"

She sighed. "It's not like that, Chrissy. Don't try to turn this into something romantic."

"I guess I just don't see where his motivation is if he doesn't have feelings for you."

Mical shrugged. "He's a decent guy."

"Decent guys say, 'Oh, sorry to hear that,' and move on with their lives. They don't propose marriage."

"Can we not talk about this right now?"

Chrissy nodded, biting into one of the cookies as she set the plate on the table. "I can't imagine how hard this all has been for you. I start crying just thinking about it—but—it's not about me—and

I know I don't have nearly the—I don't know. I'm just...I'm sorry."

Mical nodded. Chrissy had no need to explain.

Chrissy left a few minutes after Peyton arrived, when she realized they would be talking paperwork and living arrangements instead of something she might find more interesting like wedding preparations.

Peyton had drawn up the basic layout of his house to give Mical a better idea of what it would be like. They couldn't move in right away—it would take another month or two for the paperwork to go through, so Mical would stay at her house until the sale was finalized. She just hoped it wasn't taken from her before then. *I wonder how quickly banks move in on things like this.*

If they knew she was planning to list it, perhaps they would be lenient.

She heard the familiar buzz of her phone, but ignored it as she forced herself to grow accustomed to the changes that would take place in just a few weeks. *I am so tired of change.*

A key jingled in the lock and the door creaked open. It was a sound Mical had heard many times before, in the months before her father had begun his insanity—before everything became unbearable.

No, Mical corrected her own thoughts; *it was unbearable before that, too.*

Mical was so wrapped in her memories that it took a moment for her to realize the opening of the door hadn't been part of them. A shadow covered the papers on the table, forcing her to look up to discover the source.

Davey's frown lifted into a smile as her eyes reached him. "Mical," he said, his voice soft.

Mical turned away. She looked at Peyton for a sign he saw it too. A sign she wasn't completely insane.

The arms that wrapped her in warmth told her she wasn't.

Peyton stood, his own shock beginning to wear off. "You're...alive?"

Davey kissed Mical's forehead before responding. "Of course." His eyes scanned the paperwork on the table: the house design, unfiled marriage license, and directions to city hall. He stepped back, releasing Mical. "Sorry to disappoint."

Mical's entire body shook as he left her standing on her own.

Peyton seemed torn.

"Please go," Mical choked out. Her eyes were on Davey, but her words were aimed at Peyton.

She barely perceived his nod. He collected the paperwork in one large, messy pile, and walked out.

Mical closed the gap between herself and Davey. Trembling with uncertainty, she placed a hand on his cheek. "You're real," she whispered. "You're here."

He responded with silence.

Why is it so difficult to come up with words to say this? She slipped her other hand into his, craving the comfort it usually offered. *I'm sorry.*

Davey's eyes lowered. "If you want a divorce, just tell me."

For a moment, she couldn't speak. "I..." her voice faltered. *Just say it, Mical.* She looked away, her cheeks growing pink.

Davey put a hand on her jawline and gently turned her face up to his once more. "I don't want it—but it's not right to force you to stay."

"You're not."

Davey's eyes remained fixed on hers, searching. "Peyton...?"

She shook her head. "I thought you were dead, Davey."

"So you moved on."

"No! I—" She frowned, fighting the words that tried to escape.

"I love you," he said softly.

She relaxed a little. "I..." *Say it. Speak the words. This shouldn't be that hard.*

Davey smiled down at her. "I know."

She smiled a little, relieved. "Peyton is..."

"He's going to be okay," Davey said.

She nodded. "But what I mean is, he is, or I mean, he isn't—you know...anything."

Davey nodded.

"Father is going to tell you that isn't the case. He just doesn't want to see us happy."

"Are we happy, Mical?"

He didn't mean for the question to sting as it did; she knew that. She looked away.

"Mical?"

She shrugged.

"I don't think we are, Mical. But I think we can be. Tell me how to fix this."

She shook her head. "It's not you, Davey. It's me." The cliché line never felt more appropriate.

He put an arm around her. "I forgive you."

She shook her head. This was too big. He couldn't forgive it as easily as he seemed to want to.

"I mean that, Mical."

"And you're not going to...try to convince me that I should be a better person—that I should...you know..."

Davey shook his head again. "That isn't something I could pressure you into."

She nodded. "Are you terribly disappointed? You married me because you thought I was a Christian."

Davey gave her a sidelong look, raising one eyebrow in skepticism. "You think that was the only reason? I married you because you were you, and I loved you. Nothing has changed. You are still you, and I still love you."

Tears came to her eyes, as she realized just how little she deserved this man.

Davey looked concerned. "Mically?"

She needed him to admit it. She needed him to have this one fault. "You were only interested in me after I said I was a Christian," she insisted.

Davey shook his head. "I only *showed* interest after that point. I was interested long before then. I just felt I had to hide it."

She lowered her eyes and stepped back. "I'm sorry, Davey. I am so sorry."

"I'm not sorry I married you, Mical. No one will ever make me say I am."

"I don't understand why not," she said, her voice quiet.

He chuckled. "You can't get rid of me that easily."

She smiled and kissed him. "I wouldn't want to." *Say it, say it, say it,* rang through her head like a chant. She slipped her hand through his. "Davey?"

He nodded to show that he was listening. "Hmm?"

"I..." again, her voice faltered, and the words did not come. *Three simple words. He already knows, but he needs to hear it. He deserves to hear it. Say it, say it, say it...* "Davey, I love you." She swallowed when they were finally out.

He smiled and held her close. He stepped back a moment later, wincing slightly.

"Davey?"

"I'm fine," he promised. "It's my rib—but it's healing." He lowered his gaze to her stomach to see what had bumped him. He looked up a moment later, and his eyes grew smaller as his smile grew. "Really?"

Her smile matched his and she nodded. "I wanted to tell you as soon as I found out," she said, her words coming out unevenly as she struggled with happy tears.

He held her close again.

Chapter 17

Davey blinked as his eyes took in the darkness. He turned to the clock on the dresser. *Three fifteen. What woke me?* He tried to remember where his mind had wandered before he woke up. *Abigail was there...* Davey turned to the form beside him. *But Mical is here,* his conscience scolded him: for the dream, but more for the part of him that wished it had been real.

In an attempt to focus on his wife and their marriage, it had been weeks since he'd seen Abigail. The distance hadn't helped much.

Mical moved, curling up more. Her back was to him, and he could see her muscles tighten. He placed a hand on her shoulder. "Mical?"

She let out a small whimper and curled farther in.

Davey sat up. Fear of hurting her kept him from gathering her in his arms, but he stood and knelt by her side of the bed.

Mical's eyes were shut tightly, her forehead scrunched, and her cheeks were wet with tears.

He placed a hand on her arm. "Mical, what hurts?"

She took a moment to respond.

Davey reached for his phone, which was plugged in and resting on the nightstand, and scrolled his contacts list until he found the doctor's number.

"It's—" her voice cracked. "It's the baby," she whispered. "Something's wrong with the baby." She looked up at him, and her entire body trembled.

"It'll be okay, Mically," Davey said as he held the phone to his ear. A night nurse answered. "My wife is having pains. She's pregnant. Um, I think about five months?" He looked questioningly at Mical.

She made no attempt to confirm the guess.

"That's right. I think it's her stomach. No, I don't think she can talk right now. Yes. Okay—thanks." He hung up. "We're going in, Mical." He dropped the phone and placed both arms under Mical. She was a little heavier than he'd expected, and he took a moment to recover his balance before bringing her to the car.

Hours later, Mical rested on the hospital bed. Her eyes were vacant as she stared in the direction of the muted TV in the corner. Davey rubbed the back of his wife's hand as he sat beside her. Mical's tears had dried; Davey's hadn't yet arrived.

A nurse hesitantly entered the room. "Mr. and Mrs. Blake?"

Davey acknowledged her with a nearly imperceptible nod. Mical didn't move.

"I—I'm sorry," the nurse said, "but we have some paperwork…"

Everything from the past few hours melded together in his mind. His hand was sore from Mical's grip during the birth. Sweat still rested on Mical's forehead and mixed into her hair, and her fingers, still interlaced with his, trembled slightly.

"Can it wait?"

The nurse lowered her eyes as she brought the clipboard forward. "I'm afraid not."

Davey balled his fist before accepting the papers.

The nurse set a pen on the table beside Mical and left the room.

He filled out his portion. With a hoarse voice, he told Mical where her name was needed. "Mical? They want to know the—" his voice cracked, and he swallowed before continuing. "The baby's name."

For a moment, Mical's eyes seemed to fill with tears once again. "I'd been calling her Angel," she whispered.

Davey nodded. *That's too appropriate. Did she know?* He wrote "Angel Blake" on the certificate.

He put the filled-out forms on the table and watched Mical. She was hurting, he knew, but hiding it well.

Mical's attention had returned to the TV. The patient in the bed beyond the curtain was just waking up. Davey looked at the clock. He'd be late for work. *No, I just won't go at all today.*

She turned to face him. "The doctors were right." Her voice was barely audible, and Davey hardly registered her words.

"What?"

"Mom had difficult pregnancies—all three of us. She almost lost Jonathan. When I learned that, I was worried for me and Mira." She looked at their hands. "Mira's fine. I'm the weak one."

173

Davey was too tired to understand, but Mical continued.

"I went to at least five doctors, and they all said the same thing—they said I would never have children." Her voice was unnaturally peaceful. "My body couldn't handle it, they said. And they were right. Now there's just one more thing to add to your list."

Davey let out a breath of restrained emotions. "What list?"

"Your list of all my misdeeds. This is just another thing you'll have to forgive me for."

He flexed his fingers and Mical's hand fell away. Davey hesitated only a moment before walking out of the room.

He paced the hall. *Abigail would never be so...so guilt-driven and insecure. She wouldn't be afraid to let her feelings be known.*

Especially to him.

He didn't try to stop the comparison or the happy memories that almost let him forget the rest of that morning.

Abigail's ever-ready laughter filled his ears. Her sweet voice, gentle and unassuming, spoke of her passions, fears, and joys.

She had been through just as much as Mical had. Where Mr. Benson attacked with words, Nathan had used fists.

Abigail's may even have been worse, though Mical had dealt with hers for longer. Abigail's had gotten to a point where she had tried to run.

Mical was hesitant to leave even when given a clear way out.

Something in the back of Davey's mind reminded him that there was more to Mical's story. She had stayed for her siblings; if it was herself she had been concerned about, she would have been gone years earlier.

It wasn't a fair conclusion to say one was worse than the other. It wasn't even a fair comparison.

Equal amounts of pain and hurt, then, Davey decided. But that wasn't the point.

The real difference was in the way they each were dealing with the pain and hurt.

Mical was mistrustful, even now. After years of Chrissy's unconditional friendship, Mira's love, and Jonathan's brotherly protection, she couldn't believe in something as simple as love. After every promise Davey knew to give—every reworded assurance that he still cared for her and still forgave her—none of it would ever be enough.

Abigail had lived in seclusion and torment for the last five years, yet the moment she'd seen Davey she accepted him as a friend.

As that friendship grew, perhaps she had begun to think of him as more.

There had been moments—moments when Abigail's delightful stories and the scents of her cooking combined to make him forget he had a wife waiting at home—when he would wonder how their lives would be if they could stay like that forever. What would things be like if they had met each other first, before Nathan and before Mical?

It would be like his parent's relationship was. It would be everything he had been hoping for—and would never have—with Mical.

But what's stopping us from having that now? He'd already offered Mical a divorce. He could reword it; he could tell her he *wanted* one.

That might even give Mical some happiness, if that was possible. She could live independently if she wanted—or she could go back to Peyton.

Davey would have Abigail...and he would have her little one.

I could still be a father.

The thought alone was enough to bring him out of the hallway and into the lobby. He made it to the front seat of his truck before his conscience kicked in.

What am I doing? He slammed a fist on the dash. He didn't ask why; he knew why. He wasn't meant to have a happy ending.

When the fairydust settles, everything becomes clear. Happy endings don't exist.

But mine could. If I wasn't too much of a coward to make it happen.

He put the car in Drive and left the parking lot with no clear goal in mind. He wouldn't go after Abigail, as much as he wanted to, but he needed to get away.

Even if he could leave—even if freedom from him would give Mical joy—even if Abigail could be the wife he'd been dreaming of—he would forever be haunted by his mistakes.

"I told Mical that marrying her wasn't a mistake," he said to the steering wheel. "I told her no one could make me say it. But here I am saying it, and the only person forcing me to is myself."

He slammed his fist once again, hitting the edge of the steering wheel this time. "I hate this! We're broken! I hate that she doesn't see You the way I do—doesn't even believe You exist!" He was yelling now. "You're all powerful. Couldn't you have spared our child? You would have had her with you eventually anyway. You couldn't even give us one week?"

Would a week have made it any easier?

"Her whole life, then. To You, that *is* like a week. Why did You take her?" Curse words flung from his mouth as tears found his cheeks. "It could have been a miracle!" he screeched. "It could have—she would have—she might have believed." His tone grew quieter at the realization. The loss had taken more than just their child.

How could they ever be the same? How would *he* ever be the same? Even as strong as his faith had been days before, he found himself questioning God. Not His existence, but His goodness.

"When I was in distress, I sought the Lord; at night I stretched out untiring hands, and I would not be comforted."

Tears burned his cheeks as he recounted the words of the Psalmist.

"Has God forgotten to be merciful? Has he in anger withheld his compassion?" He buried his head in his hands. "You are the God who performs miracles. So where," he cursed, "where is our miracle?"

He was out of things to say. Arguing with his invisible creator wouldn't do any good. His Angel was gone.

I will consider all your works and meditate on all your mighty deeds. Your ways, God, are holy.

And wholly incomprehensible to me.

His words ceased for another reason: quiet acceptance. He hadn't met Abigail first because he wasn't meant to.

We'd be happy. It wouldn't take much to move from loving each other as friends to...more.

But it would be wrong.

"I chose Mical. Nothing has changed. I still choose Mical...every day."

Davey drove back to the hospital and walked to Mical's room.

She didn't acknowledge him when he walked in, so he sat beside her without a word. He watched her for a moment. "Do you have a list for me?"

She shook her head, not looking in his direction. "What would I put on it if I did? I'm the one who keeps messing up."

"Mical," Davey said, his tone gentle but firm.

She looked at him, seeming to expect a rebuke. Her eyebrows drew together and her pupils darted to and from his own.

He slipped her hand through his and just held it for a moment. *How much should I tell her?*

She turned away again. "You would have a child if it wasn't for me."

"No, Mical."

"It's true. I know it is. It was *my* body that caused this. Maybe it's God punishing me."

"*No*, Mical," he said, his voice more insistent. "He doesn't do that."

"To you, He doesn't. You're His beloved one— His child, right? So if it wasn't for me, you'd have a real family. He wouldn't take your little one from you without a reason."

How do I help her see what You're like, Papa? I don't even know what You're like.

She let out a shaky breath. "He's been punishing me for a while, I think."

"He loves you, Mical."

"No. It's not possible. He—He wouldn't take my baby if He did."

Davey wrapped his arm behind her shoulders and brought her close to him. He slipped his hand out of hers and ran his fingers through her hair and along the side of her cheek. He kissed her forehead. His words came slowly and carefully, re-membering each word of the verse as he spoke: "But you, O Lord, are a God merciful and gracious, slow to anger and abounding in steadfast love and faithfulness."

"He also said," Mical countered, "I love those who love me, and those who seek me diligently find me."

Davey smiled at her willingness to discuss the once-forbidden subject. For her, he was only just beginning to realize, it had always been a reminder of what she had done to him. It added to the guilt she was already feeling.

He nodded in response to the verse. "And He does love those who love Him. But that verse doesn't say He *doesn't* love those who don't follow Him. In this is love, not that we have loved God but that he loved us."

Mical's voice grew faint as she nodded slightly. "You really believe that...that He's like that?"

"Sometimes," Davey said. "When things like this happen, it's harder. It doesn't *feel* like He's loving us right now. But faith is not based on feelings—which is probably a good thing."

"Because feelings don't last."

"Unless you work at them."

"Are we working at them?" Mical's expression was filled with hope as she waited for his response.

"We will," he promised.

Chapter 18

Mical read over the chapter again. She'd read it before at least twice, and had been told the story again and again when she was growing up, but there was something different about it now. It had never felt so...real before.

Davey stirred next to her and rolled over, pulling more of the covers with him.

She smiled. *Blanket hog. One of his few flaws...and he doesn't even know he's doing it.* The usual guilt that settled in her stomach at thoughts like those was replaced with delightful butterflies.

She watched her husband sleeping calmly for what must have been the first time in two weeks. Unable to resist the touch she'd craved in the months he'd been away, she set a hand on his arm, rubbing gently.

She took in a deep breath, loving his scent.

Davey turned to face her and offered a sleepy smile in greeting.

"Good morning, darling," she said. "I didn't mean to wake you. It's your day to sleep in."

He sat up. "You didn't—" His hand wasn't quick enough to cover his yawn, and he smiled as it released. "It's okay."

"You looked like you were peaceful," she said, an apology in her voice.

He nodded. "Sleep often is."

"Not for you. Not lately."

Davey put an arm around her. He noticed the book on her lap. His eyes met hers, searching.

"I've...I've been reconsidering," she said. She looked down. "I don't expect you to believe me. I'm the boy who cried wolf; I know."

He chuckled. "I rather like that way of putting it. But that's not how I see you anymore."

"I know," she said with a small smile.

He brought her closer to him and kissed her gently. Her eyes closed in contentment as their lips met.

Davey released a moment later. "What's your favorite part so far?" he asked as they parted.

"This one," she said. "You and me; together like this."

"I actually meant in...never mind. This is my favorite part, too...so far."

She grinned. "Would you read to me, Davey?" Mical handed him the Bible.

"What part did you stop at?" he asked, letting it fall open in his lap.

Mical smiled. "It doesn't matter. Read me one of the parts you love best." She leaned her head against his shoulder and watched as he flipped through the pages of the worn Bible.

Davey opened it to a section her mother had covered in notes and highlights. The knowledge that both her mother and her husband shared a love of the passage brought a warm feeling to her, and her smile grew.

Davey began to read in his low, clear voice, and Mical listened in pure joy. Her eyes closed as images of the scene painted across her mind.

It was the story of Mary and Martha. Davey came to the part where Martha scolded her sister for not helping.

Mical could see herself doing the same to Jonathan—and was pretty sure that she had at least once. He was always wandering off to socialize when there was still work to be done.

Davey continued, reading about Jesus' critique of Martha.

Mical's nose scrunched. She had wanted to like the story, but even just that morning she had found several other passages that were more beautiful. The Bible was filled with tales of "miracles" and proof of people's love; why would Davey pick such a dull story to read to her?

Davey stopped reading and looked at her. "Why the face?"

She shrugged, not wanting to hurt his feelings. This was obviously an important chapter to him, even if she couldn't see the reason.

"You can tell me," he assured her.

"It's just...I'm wondering why you picked that part. I guess I just don't see, um, the appeal?" She winced slightly. *Well, being tactful didn't happen.*

Davey chuckled. "You mean because it's just a family feud and nothing special?"

She nodded.

"It's special to me, because...well, here. Your mom wrote a note in the margin that explains it better than I could." He handed her the book, his finger resting just below the handwritten words.

Mical read it carefully, her own finger tracing the slightly indented, thoughtfully written sentences.

Jesus doesn't need us to have everything together when we go to Him—doesn't even want it! Just craves us. How beautiful.

She read it through again. The idea wasn't a new one. The presentation wasn't even very original. Maybe it was the early morning happiness, or having Davey so near to her. Maybe it was that, for the first time in weeks, she didn't feel a need to cry, break something, or both.

She read it a third time and let the meaning of the words really take hold.

If He existed, and if her mother had been right, Jesus *craved* her. Her! Broken, battered, and cynical as she was, He wanted her—not some picture perfect copy of her.

But that was a big 'if', and her marriage might not survive another almost-conversion. She said nothing as she passed the Bible back to Davey.

"Well?" He asked, watching her expression.

"It's nice," she said with a small shrug.

Davey blinked; he had read more in her features than she had intended. "Just...'nice'?"

She lowered her chin and looked at him from the side, warning him to drop the subject. *I can't say more, Davey. Not right now.*

"Okay," he said, correctly interpreting her look. "Are you hungry?"

"Of course," she said, laughing as his stomach betrayed his own answer. "What would you like for breakfast?"

"I'm sure we can find something together," he smiled as he stepped out of bed.

She followed him to the kitchen and pulled a few pans out of the cupboard as he opened the fridge.

"I'm thinking eggs," he said.

Mical made a face. "We've had eggs for the past week," she protested. "Can't we have something else? Like...like your awesome caramel rolls?"

Davey chuckled. "Didn't you just hear my stomach tell you it wants food *now*? Besides, eggs are healthy for you. Unless you have too many—but nothing is healthy if you have too much of it. Even salad. Even celery."

"Really?"

"Okay, that's probably not true...but I like to think it is anyway. I can only handle a little bit of those things."

She giggled. "Fine, we'll have eggs."

"I'll make them special, don't worry." Davey pulled out some seasonings and dug parsley, broccoli, garlic, and cheese from the fridge.

Mical looked at the ingredients somewhat skeptically. "What are you going to do with those?"

"Add them to the eggs, of course." He handed her the broccoli.

She shrugged and started washing it.

He chopped a few cloves of garlic, and cut the cheese into small blocks. "Remember when you did this to the cheeseburger cheese?"

She blinked. "You knew those were going to be cheeseburgers?"

"You'd pressed the meat into patties. What else would it have been?" He laughed. "But you looked so lost with those cheese cubes...I had to give you another option."

She sprinkled water in his face. "You're horrible."

"I was being kind!"

Mical laughed. "Being kind by being sneaky doesn't count."

"So all those anonymous donations people give don't mean a thing to you?"

"What anonymous donations?" she asked.

"Any," he said, laughing. "People give them out all the time, you know. Are you saying that means nothing because they haven't made it obvious who the gift is coming from?"

"I'm done with this," she said. "It's a silly topic, and I'm not going to play this game with you anymore."

He grinned, believing he had won the conversation.

She moved the broccoli to a cutting board and aimed the remaining water from her fingers at him.

"There's no need to be a sore loser now," Davey chuckled.

"I didn't lose. I'm dry; you're wet. I consider that a win."

He shrugged and started cutting the parsley.

"Shouldn't you be cooking the eggs?" Mical asked as her own stomach made a loud complaint.

"Not yet," Davey said, shaking his head. "And I thought *I* was the impatient one. How's that broccoli coming?" He looked over her shoulder.

"Fine. You gave me the hard job, though."

"I did?"

She nodded. "It's much easier to cut garlic and parsley."

"Oh—then here," he offered her the cutting board he'd been using.

"Not *now*. I'm almost done!"

"Exactly—so there won't be much left for me to do. I consider *that* a win."

Mical laughed.

Davey cracked a few eggs into a bowl, then dropped in the parsley and garlic and mixed it together. "Whenever you're done with your difficult task, the broccoli can join these guys," he said.

She pulled her lips tight and gave an almost smirk as she cut the final pieces and dumped them into the bowl.

Davey stirred the mixture, then poured it into a frying pan and turned on the heat. He waited for the eggs to start cooking.

"You know," Mical said slowly, "I'm part of your family now."

"Really?"

She elbowed him.

"Hey—hot pan here."

"It's not hot yet," she laughed.

"Fine," Davey agreed. "But it's messy, at least."

Mical rolled her eyes.

"Okay, so, as of this moment, you're part of my family. I guess the last half a year didn't count, but that's cool. I'm glad to know it's official now."

"Just listen," she said. "You told us before that you couldn't share the recipe of your caramel rolls because it was a family thing. So...I think it's time you shared it."

"Want to know a secret?" he asked.

"That was kind of my entire point here."

Davey chuckled. "Okay. The real reason I couldn't share the recipe is because I don't have one."

"What do you mean? You've made them several times."

"Yes, but always without a recipe."

"So it's in your head."

"Right. Sort of. I just know what it's supposed to look like and feel like and the general idea of what goes into it."

"So...it's in your head."

Davey laughed. "I suppose you could word it like that."

"I just did. Twice." A mischievous grin spread across Mical's face. "So...let's make them together, and then it can be in my head, too."

"You're really not going to let this go, are you?"

"Does the thought of cooking with me scare you that much that you feel the need to keep postponing it?" she asked, offering him her sweetest smile.

Davey pointed to the pan of eggs on the stove. "What do you call this?" he asked.

"I call it you cooking while I do the manual labor."

"Really? Manual labor is what you're going with?"

She shrugged. "I think it fits."

"I think you need to look up that term in a dictionary." He laughed and started pulling ingredients out of the cupboards.

Mical grinned when she saw what he was doing. "What dictionary are you looking in? I haven't found any that define two words at once. And I promise you the definition of manual plus the definition of labor will not be the same as the definition of manual labor."

Davey shrugged. "I'm sure you could find the definition somewhere if you really wanted to." He got the hand mixer from the cupboard.

"So...are you going to teach me anything here or am I just going to stand around and watch this one, too? By the way, your eggs are burning."

Davey ran to the stove and stirred the pan. "They're not burning," he said after a moment. "Don't be so dramatic." He winked.

She laughed. "They look brown to me."

"Brown, yes. Not black. There's a big difference."

"Both are colors eggs should never be, you know."

"Right. Eggs should be purple and green and blue."

Mical blinked. "What kind of eggs are you eating?"

"Oh, you weren't talking about the shells, were you?"

She shook her head. "Besides—brown eggshells happen naturally. It's the bright white that's not normal. If the inside of your eggs is purple or blue, there's a problem. If they're green, you've been reading way too much Dr. Seuss."

"No such thing," Davey grinned.

She shrugged. "If you say so."

"Okay...I'll try to teach you this," he finally relented, "if only because I can't seem to figure out where you've stashed the measuring cups, and they're a little bit important."

Mical laughed. "That was my plan all along. I've hidden them in the dishwasher." She pulled the lids off the flour, salt, and sugar. "What comes first?"

"All in good time, my dear," he smiled.

"Now isn't a good time?"

Davey laughed. "It's not a perfect time. It'll do in a pinch."

"You are so weird."

"And you love me for it."

"Sometimes."

Davey frowned, but Mical knew it wasn't a serious expression. "You only love me sometimes?"

"I only love you for your weirdness sometimes. I always love you." It was so much easier to admit it now.

He grinned. "I know."

Mical's phone vibrated. She smiled at the name on the screen and held it up to her ear. "Hi, Abigail!" She walked out of the kitchen as they started to talk.

She sat on the couch, tucking her legs underneath her. "Oh, we were just making breakfast. Did

Davey ever make you his caramel rolls when he was staying with you?"

"No...but I'm intrigued by the idea."

Mical turned to the opening of the kitchen. "Why didn't you make them for her, Davey?"

Davey chuckled. "I didn't do much cooking there," he said.

"Well, you should come over for them sometime. He was about to teach me how. It's a big secret of his." She giggled.

Abigail laughed. "I actually called to invite you here...but I guess I missed the chance to feed you breakfast."

"Why don't you come here? Davey—" she covered the phone with her hand as she turned toward the kitchen again, "Abigail can come over, can't she?"

Davey chuckled. "Of course, Mical."

She grinned and spoke into the phone again. "It's settled then. You're coming."

Abigail's smile showed in her tone. "Thanks, Mical! I'll be there soon."

Mical smiled, grateful for her relatively new friend. She felt as close to Abigail in the two months she'd known her as she was to Chrissy—and that friendship had taken years to form.

Shared experiences do that, though. Abigail was the one friend who understood, from experience, the pain of losing a child. *Papa...please protect her little one.*

Chapter 19

Abigail had started calling Mical instead of Davey after they'd met each other, and he didn't mind.

As much as he loved Mical—and as delighted as he was to see her changing her opinion about his Papa—the temptation to move to someone who was already much stronger in her faith was still a very real one.

He had been wrong to spend as much time as he had with her. He hadn't done anything beyond talking—but that didn't mean it was okay. If it was, it would have been much easier to tell Mical.

He did tell her, eventually.

She lowered her eyes as she listened to the confession.

"I'm so sorry, Mical. I shouldn't have kept this from you. And I shouldn't have let it happen in the first place."

She looked at him. "Thank you for telling me, Davey." She kissed him gently. "I love you."

His eyebrows moved higher. "You're not upset?"

She shook her head. "I know why you felt the way you did. And I know you don't feel that way anymore." She smiled. "Besides...it's not like you got engaged or something." She giggled softly.

Davey thought about her 'relationship' with Peyton as he sat in the room of monitors at his new job.

It had been a one-sided romance. Peyton had moved in on the possibility of one when there seemed to be an opportunity to do so.

Most guys would have asked the girl on a date and started from there. In a normal circumstance, Davey knew Peyton would have done the same. But this wasn't a normal circumstance, and he had jumped to wedding plans instead—because Mical was expecting a baby and losing her house at the same time.

Maybe there's some good in that creep, after all. Davey smiled a little as he waited for some activity. *At least he watched over Mically when I couldn't be there.*

In one of the security cameras, Davey could see raindrops painting the window. Policing a local mall wasn't ideal. It mainly involved sitting in front of TV screens, and the most he'd had to do in the past month was confiscate a pair of sneakers from a would-be shoplifter.

Sometimes he got to walk around in his uniform and look menacing, which was fun for the first half hour.

It also paid less than he'd been making with Mr. Benson, but it was worth the cut.

Though, working for him isn't really an option anymore.

He knew after his conversation with the Ellsworth police officer that he had enough evidence to put Mr. Benson in prison, and sometimes he'd been tempted to do it.

It didn't seem right to let him run free after all he'd done. Mr. Benson may not have been the murderer, but he was just as guilty as one.

Still, something told him it would be better for Mical if he left things as they were.

And now he's gone, so what difference would it make? His memory is tarnished enough without adding murder charges to it.

Jonathan had found him after he'd done it, and now he was forced to live with that image the rest of his life.

Papa, I would love to know one good thing that man ever did. Mical had told him he was a good man when she was younger—before he'd lost his wife and retaliated in anger against his children.

He smiled at the thought of his beautiful wife. She had changed so much since he had come home. *She changed after she met Abigail, really.* She was happier and more willing to listen.

Mical was still her feisty self, and he was glad. She was *his* feisty one.

She'd hit me if she knew that's how I thought of her. She didn't belong to anyone...but at the same time, she *was* his—just as much as he was hers.

He smiled again. That morning she had admitted that she had been thinking about God and the Bible, and that she might have to reconsider what she had initially thought. She had been contemplating it for a while. Davey had found her reading the Bible or praying when she didn't think he was watching, and sometimes she asked him to read to her.

She wasn't trying to deceive him this time. He had no doubt that, this time, she was sincere.

Thank You, Papa. Thank You for my beautiful wife. Thank You for leading her to You...even if Your timing didn't match with mine.

God's timing seldom did match with his—but it was always better than his would have been. In this case, he couldn't help but feel that a lot of pain would have been avoided if, just this once, God had listened to him instead of the other way around, but he knew there must have been a reason.

I know 'everything happens for a reason' isn't anywhere in the Bible, he sent up another internal prayer, *but it still seems true. At least...everything that happens can be used for a purpose. Maybe that's a better—more biblical—way of wording it. Everything can be used for good. That's in there somewhere.*

He chuckled to himself, and was glad today was one of the days in the booth. It wouldn't help the mall's image to have a security guard laughing at nothing when others could see and hear him.

Aside from the rain and a handful of shoppers, the monitors were completely calm. He glanced at his watch. *Three more hours. Then I can go home.*

Someday, he would find a job he actually enjoyed. For now, this was paying the bills that had been piling up while he was away.

Mical had done her best. She'd taken a job at a gas station and was working as often as she could, but the low wage she received wouldn't have been enough to keep the debt away even if she'd been working full time.

He convinced her to quit soon after he'd come home. She needed the time to grieve—and he knew she wanted to focus on her schoolwork.

She'd been getting behind on that, too.

He made it his mission to be there to help her in any way he could.

For now, that meant working a menial job that paid the bills. That's what men do—at least, that's what his father had taught him, and Sammy had repeated the idea several times.

He looked at his watch again. *Two hours and fifty five minutes until I can see my darling.* Davey chuckled again. *This mushiness really needs to stop.*

He doubted Mical would mind if she knew, though. She would pretend to, of course—that was only natural for her.

Everything about her was returning to what he had first fallen in love with—and, somehow, becoming even better than he could have imagined.

His phone, lying on the table next to his luke-warm mug of coffee, started to buzz. He glanced at it. *Abigail?* He didn't answer it, only because he was on the clock. He'd listen to the message soon enough.

When break time came and his replacement arrived, he went outside to see what she'd needed.

"Davey, um, it's time. I tried Mical but she's not answering...I'm scared. Your parents are gone and I don't know where to go..."

Davey hurried back to the monitor room. "Hey, Jason...would you mind covering the rest of my shift? I promise I'll make it up to you anytime you need it."

"Sure, man, whatever," Jason said, taking a drink from Davey's mug. He frowned in distaste. "Your coffee got cold."

Davey chuckled. "Sorry. And thanks."

He grabbed his keys from the table and ran to his truck, dialing Mical's number on the way.

"Hey honey," she said, sounding as out of breath as he was feeling. "I just got a message from Abigail—"

"I did too."

"I'm picking her up. Meet me at the hospital?"

"I'll be there," he promised.

He was there before Mical, so he waited in the lobby area. He started fidgeting seconds after he sat down, so he stood and began to pace instead.

Mical and Abigail entered, Abigail leaning on her for support. Mical gave a real smile and Abigail forced one when they saw Davey. A moment later, Abigail grimaced and put a hand on her stomach.

Someone directed her to her room, and Davey returned to pacing. He knew enough not to follow them in, but he was nervous. Abigail's baby had been through a lot...and the last time he'd been at the hospital hadn't ended well. *Please let her little one be healthy,* he prayed.

He paced. He sat. He tried to sleep. It wasn't until hours had passed, after the sun had gone down and his stomach was past the point of complaints, that Mical joined him in the waiting room.

"It's the most beautiful little girl," she said, her eyes glistening with unshed tears. He couldn't decipher if they were from joy or sadness; perhaps it was a mix of both. "Abigail wants you to meet her." She slipped her arm through his and led her to the room.

Abigail was sitting up, cradling her baby girl. Her hair was desperately in need of a brush and sweat caused it to cling to her forehead, and her cheeks were still pink from the effort, but she was smiling.

Davey's attention turned to the tiny baby in her arms, and he let out a very unmanly "Aww."

Mical giggled. "What's her name?" she asked.

Abigail turned to them for the first time since they had come in. "That's something I wanted to talk to you about."

Mical looked at Davey, and the way her eyebrows drew together assured him she was as confused as he was.

"It's...well... I want to give her the best life possible," Abigail said slowly, her eyes returning to her baby. "I love her so much more than I expected to—so this is really hard...but that also proves that it's important."

"What is it, Abigail?" Mical asked.

"I know this is a lot to ask...but I can't think of anyone I'd trust more."

"For what?" Davey prodded, knowing she needed help to force the question out.

She took a deep breath. After a moment, she looked up. "I can't be a father *and* a mother for her...and I want her to have both. Would you...would you adopt her?"

Mical and Davey looked at one another for a moment.

"Do you really mean it?" Mical asked, her voice nearly a whisper.

Abigail nodded. "I couldn't ask for anyone better."

Davey smiled. "We would be honored to, Abigail."

"Thank you," she said, turning back to her—their—baby. "So it's up to you what her name is." She smiled.

"Can I hold her?" Mical whispered the question.

"Of course," Abigail said, though she seemed reluctant to let her go.

Mical, though unused to babies, held the sleeping child close and rocked her instinctively. "She's precious," she said, her voice still a whisper.

Abigail smiled. "You will make the best mom," she said.

"What's your middle name?" Mical asked.

"Marie," Abigail answered. "But please don't name her that..."

Mical glanced at Davey.

"I'm terrible with names," he said, knowing she had something in mind.

"What about AnnaMarie?"

Chapter 20

"Are you sure you want to do this?" Mical asked as she picked up a small statue from her father's desk.

Jonathan nodded. "I have no desire to live in this place alone," he said. "It was too big even when you, Mira, and Dad were living here with me."

She nodded, putting another meaningless item in a "donate" box.

Mira held up a picture frame. "Remember this?" The three Benson children were on a beach, smiling. Their pants were rolled up to their knees, but the bottoms had still been soaked.

Jonathan looked at it and shook his head. "I look like a baby."

Mical took the photo from Mira. "You were two," she said. "Your birthday was a month before." She remembered the day, no matter how much she tried to forget it.

"Dad took us there to distract us," Mira said, her voice soft from the memory, "when Mom went to the hospital."

"From our smiles, I guess it worked," Jonathan commented.

Mical shrugged. "It did for a little while." She set the picture in the "donate" box.

Mira fished it out. "You can't get rid of this," she said, holding it close. "I want it."

"I didn't know Dad had *any* photos of us," Jonathan commented as he added another pile of trinkets to the box.

"Yeah, well, he certainly could have found a more recent one," Mical mumbled. "If he'd cared to."

Jonathan shrugged. "I guess."

"I think it's sweet he kept it," Mira said.

"Nothing about Father was sweet," Mical snapped. *He kept it because it was the last day he loved us.*

Her siblings didn't respond.

Jonathan dropped another pile into the box. "Who knew Dad was such a hoarder?"

I wish he would stop calling him that. He wasn't a dad to us—at least, not after Mom died. That's an earned title, and he lost it.

"Those were ours when we were little," Mira said, pulling out a little toy truck. "This was yours, Jonathan."

"I remember that one," he nodded.

"And this was mine," she pulled out a doll and hugged it.

Aiden walked in, carrying another box of things. "I have more for you to go through," he said, his tone far too cheerful.

"Oh joy," Mical muttered. "Let's just toss it all. Well, all except what Jonathan needs for his new place. Some furniture, the things from your room, and whatever food is here."

Jonathan shrugged. "I'm not the only reason we're going through these things."

"No?" she shook her head. "You're delusional if you think we'd be organizing this junk if you hadn't asked us to."

"It's not junk," Mira said, pulling a worn book from the box Aiden had brought.

"Don't you see, Mically?" Jonathan held up a stuffed cat that was missing all but two patches of fur.

Muffin! She reached for the favorite toy.

"He kept all our stuff," Jonathan said. "At least, he kept the import things. The sentimental ones."

"I knew I got it from somewhere," Mira smiled as she pulled items from the box. "I thought he'd sold these. You know, when he bought that awful *David* statue. Our old stuff just kind of disappeared."

Mical remembered. She had still wanted Muffin at that point, but was still afraid of her father's outbursts and didn't ask about it.

"Where did you find it?" Mira asked.

"It was in his room, on a top shelf in his closet." Aiden sat next to Mira and wrapped an arm around her. "There's more in there," he added.

"It must have meant something to him," Mira said. "He didn't keep anything else like it."

Mical looked around the room. The walls and tables were sparse; the decorations he did have were simple. *And probably cost him thousands.*

She looked at the toy in her hands. "Well, I stopped needing this thing when I was ten." She threw it back in the box. "I certainly don't need it *now*."

Mira frowned and glanced at Aiden. "He can't hurt us anymore, Mical," she said.

"Hurt *us*?" Mical's eyes narrowed as she spoke. "When did he ever hurt *us*?" She laughed, but it contained no humor.

"All the time, Mical," Mira said, not sure how to interpret her sister's words. "You don't remember? I mean...it happened up until the point you moved out."

And even after. "Oh, I remember," Mical said, her voice stiff. "I remember all the times he hurt *me*."

Mira and Jonathan exchanged a look of sympathy as she continued.

"Father called *me* names. He told *me* I would never amount to anything." She picked up the stuffed animal and squeezed it harder than necessary. "His anger never touched either of *you*. I made sure of that."

Mira hesitantly stepped closer and put a hand on Mical's arm. "I know, Mical. But that hurt, too."

"What? That he didn't give you the same attention?" Mical yanked her arm away. "Don't give me that look. I don't want your sympathy."

Mira frowned. "Mical...please listen. I hated seeing him do that to you. I was the older one. I should have taken that on; not you."

"No," Mical said firmly, throwing the stuffed cat back into the box and walked towards the door. "No one should have. It never should have happened."

"Well, I certainly can't argue with that," Aiden said.

This isn't his fight. She barely restrained herself from telling him to shut up.

"The fact is, it did happen," Aiden continued. "He hurt you, and hurt your siblings by extension. Imagine if someone tried to hurt Davey—or AnnaMarie."

She frowned. "Keep them out of this. It's not the same."

"I know it's different," Aiden said. "I know it's a different kind of pain when it's happening directly. I'm sorry it happened. I'm sorry your father abused you. It was wrong."

Mical kept her back to him as tears came to her eyes. *Davey was the only one to acknowledge it before.* Chrissy understood; Abigail was starting to. But neither had addressed it the same way.

Aidan's smile had left his voice. "I don't know what will help," he said. "But I know holding onto bitterness isn't it."

She spun to face him. "You don't know what it was like. None of you do." She hurried down the stairs before the others could see her tears.

Davey was in the kitchen, gently rocking AnnaMarie. Remnants of her latest meal painted his shirt, but with his attention on the little one he didn't seem to notice. He looked up from the baby as Mical walked in. "What happened?"

She dropped into the chair beside him. The sight of her child brought a smile, but only for a moment. "I hate this house," she said.

He nodded. "There are a lot of memories here."

"They're not *all* bad," she said. "I mean...I met you here." She smiled again, a small one. "But even that doesn't make up for the painful ones."

"I wish there was something I could have done," Davey said. "Or at least some way we could understand why it happened."

She shrugged. "It happened because Papa gave us free will. Father used it to hurt me. I used it to hurt you. There doesn't have to be a reason."

"Maybe you're right," Davey said. "A reason sure would be nice, though."

She shrugged.

"That doesn't help, does it?"

"You help," she said. "AnnaMarie does, too. And Papa definitely does. It's just...being here. *That* doesn't help."

Davey nodded.

"How did you do it every day?"

"It was a job."

"So?"

He shrugged. "I don't have the same memories you do," he said.

"I know—but he still hurt you. How could you look at him with," she focused on her hands, "with compassion?"

"I couldn't, Mical. I didn't even try to," he said. He bounced the little one.

Mical looked up. "You didn't?"

"I was civil to him," he said, "because he was my boss and my father-in-law. But I could never look at that man with anything warmer than contempt."

She smiled. "My husband is a human after all," she said with a short laugh.

He chuckled.

Mical glanced around the kitchen. The decorations hadn't changed since she'd lived there a year before. Even the spaghetti sauce stain on the wall hadn't been painted over.

"If Jonathan doesn't want them, maybe we could bring home some of these appliances," Davey suggested. "If that wouldn't...you know..."

She nodded a little. "The kitchen has good memories in it." Her face still showed pain, though.

"We can leave any time you want to," he said, watching her with an uncertain expression. "I'm sure your siblings will understand."

She nodded. "I know."

Mira tapped lightly on the kitchen wall. "Mically? Can I show you something?"

Mical hesitated, but stood. Davey followed them as they walked back to her father's office.

Jonathan and Aiden were sitting on the floor, strangely silent. Jonathan was holding a couple sheets of note paper and shaking his head. He looked up when she entered and held it up to her. "You need to read this," he said, his voice quiet.

She looked at the paper without accepting it. "What is it?"

"Just read it."

"It's from Dad," Mira said. "I think it's the last thing he wrote."

Mical frowned, but took the note. She glanced at Davey. *I'm not sure I want to see what he wrote.*

She gripped the paper without looking at it. "Why does it matter?" *Why should I care what that man said?*

"It might help you understand," Mira said. "I mean...it doesn't say why he did it. But it still might...help."

I doubt it.

Still, she sat in the desk chair and started to read. Her hand shook as she skimmed the short note.

seven, five, and barely two.
Those were the ages of
my children when I
became their only parent.

There had been so many
words meant to
encourage; trying to
show sympathy. I
can't remember even
one. There were so
many apologies—but
no one was at fault.

No one but God.

But it wasn't God who

took the punishment; it was my children.

None of the harsh words or cruel deeds were deserved.

I don't ask for forgiveness, and I know I won't be given it.

I'm getting what I deserve now.

For the first time, Mical felt something other than bitterness toward her father: compassion. *When we lost Mom, he lost the love of his life. And he lost love completely.*

Davey, who had read over her shoulder, wrapped one arm around her.

She folded up the note and set it on the desk. She kept her eyes on it as the others waited for a response.

"He loved us, Mical," Mira said, her voice gentle. "This is his way of telling us." She motioned to one of the boxes, filled with remnants of their past. "These are his way of showing it. I know it's not enough..."

"No, it's not," Mical agreed. "But it's the best he could do." She sighed.

I still don't understand, Papa. But maybe I don't have to. He had been wrong. Davey had helped her see that, but the knowledge had only added to her bitterness.

For the first time, she saw that her father had known it, too. The note wasn't an apology and it wasn't an explanation, but she chose to see it as both.

She picked up Muffin and handed the toy to her daughter.

AnnaMarie wrapped her little arms around it, and Davey put a hand on it to keep it from dropping.

My father gave me that. It was in the hospital gift shop, and he must have seen me hugging it.

Mira was right; he'd shown his love with gifts and money. That would have to be enough.

Dad, wherever you are now, I hope you know...I forgive you.

Davey and Mical Blake

Happy endings don't mean there are no difficulties. Princes and princesses don't fall in love without first overcoming poisoned apples, cursed spindles, or enchanted towers.

It's the struggles that sweeten the ending, when everything settles and joy still remains. Perhaps happily ever after was never *meant* to happen for us, but somehow, in its own way...it did.

About the Author

Books have been a part of Jansina's life for as long as she can remember. She was the kind of kid who pulled out grammar books in the summer and wrote research papers "for fun." (No joke.)

In the fall of 2011, she finished and published her first novel, *Forgotten Memories*. The summer of 2012 brought the next, *Shrouded Jewels*. Davey and Mical can be found in both.

Also in 2012, Jansina began an editing and publishing business, Rivershore Books (www.rivershorebooks.com). There are now three secondary proofreaders and an illustrator working with her, and the business continues to grow.

Jansina's next project, *Tomatoes Don't Judge,* is a story of friendship and focuses on Davey's younger brother, Robbie.

So many steps led to where she is now, and she truly feels it's what Papa (her affectionate name for God) wants her to be doing. Her goal is to honor Him in her writing and encourage other authors to do the same with their own.

Previous Stories:

Forgotten Memories
Sanisfreeda
Shrouded Jewels

Available on Amazon, Smashwords, Barnes & Noble, and Rivershore Books:

www.rivershorebooks.storenvy.com

Find Jansina Online:

thilly-little-nothings.blogspot.com
www.facebook.com/Jansina
www.twitter.com/Jansina18

Learn About Rivershore Books:

www.rivershorebooks.com
www.blog.rivershorebooks.com
rivershorebooks.proboards.com
www.facebook.com/rivershore.books
www.twitter.com/rivershorebooks

Email Jansina:

Jansina@rivershorebooks.com